THE TICKET
THAT EXPLODED

Works by William S. Burroughs
Published by Grove Press

Naked Lunch
The Ticket That Exploded
The Soft Machine
Nova Express
The Wild Boys
Word Virus: The William S. Burroughs Reader
Last Words

William S. Burroughs

THE TICKET
THAT EXPLODED

posed little time
so I'll say
　　　　　"good night"

GROVE PRESS ▫ New York

An earlier version of this novel was first published in 1962 by The Olympia Press, Paris. Part of the section entitled *silence to say good bye* appeared in *The Insect Trust Gazette*, No. 1, Summer 1964; a portion of the Appendix was published in *The International Times*, London.

Published simultaneously in Canada
Printed in the United States of America

Library of Congress Cataloging-in-Publication Data

Burroughs, William S., 1914– 1997.
    The ticket that exploded.

    Previously published: London: Calder & Boyars, 1968.
    ISBN 0-8021-5150-7
    I. Title.
PS3552.U75T487   1987   813'.54   86-33486

Grove Press
841 Broadway
New York, NY 10003

03   15 14 13 12 11 10

Acknowledgment

The sections entitled *in a strange bed* and *the black fruit* were written in collaboration with Mr. Michael Portman of London. Mr. Ian Sommerville of London pointed out the use and significance of spliced tape and all the other tape recorder experiments suggested in this book. The film experiments suggested I owe to Mr. Anthony Balch of Balch Films, London. The closing message is by Brion Gysin.

It is a long trip. We are the only riders. So that is how
we have come to know each other so well that the sound
of his voice and his image flickering over the tape recorder
are as familiar to me as the movement of my intestines the
sound of my breathing the beating of my heart. Not that
we love or even like each other. In fact murder is never
out of my eyes when I look at him. And murder is never
out of his eyes when he looks at me. Murder under a
carbide lamp in Puya rain outside it's a mighty wet place
drinking *aguardiente* with tea and canella to cut that
kerosene taste he called me a drunken son of a bitch and
there it was across the table raw and bloody as a fresh
used knife . . sitting torpid and quiescent in a canvas chair
after reading last month's Sunday comics "the jokes" he
called them and read every word it sometimes took him a
full hour by a tidal river in Mexico slow murder in his eyes
maybe ten fifteen years later I see the move he made
then he was a good amateur chess player it took up most
of his time actually but he had plenty of that. I offered to

1

play him once he looked at me and smiled and said: "You wouldn't stand a chance with me."

His smile was the most unattractive thing about him or at least it was one of the unattractive things about him it split his face open and something quite alien like a predatory mollusk looked out different well I took his queen in the first few minutes of play by making completely random moves. He won the game without his queen. I had made my point and lost interest. Panama under the ceiling fans, on the cold winds of Chimborazo, across the rubble of Lima, steaming up from the mud streets of Esmeraldas that flat synthetic vulgar CIA voice of his . . basically he was completely hard and self-seeking and thought entirely in terms of position and advantage an effective but severely limited intelligence. Thinking on any other level simply did not interest him. He was by the way very cruel but not addicted to the practice of cruelty. He was cruel if the opportunity presented itself. Then he smiled his eyes narrowed and his sharp little ferret teeth showed between his thin lips which were a blue purple color in a smooth yellow face. But then who am I to be critical few things in my own past I'd just as soon forget . .

What I am getting at is we do not like each other we simply find ourselves on the same ship sharing the same cabin and often the same bed welded together by a million shared meals and belches by the movement of intestines and the sound of breathing (he snored abominably. I turn him on his side or stomach to shut him up. He wakes and smiles in the dark room muttering "Don't get ideas") by the beating of our hearts. In fact his voice has been spliced in 24 times per second with the sound of my breathing and the beating of my heart so that my body is convinced that my breathing and heart will stop if his voice stops.

"Well," he would say with his winsome smile, "it does give a certain position of advantage."

My attempts to murder him were usually direct . . knife . . gun . . in some one elses hand of course I had no intention of getting into social difficulties . . car accident . . drowning . . once a shark surfaced in my mind as he plunged from a boat into the tidal river . . I will go to his 'aid and clutch his torn dying body in my arms like a vise he will be too weak from loss of blood to fight me off and my face will be his last picture. He always planned that *his* face should be my last picture and his plan called for cinerama film sequences featuring the Garden of Delights shows all kinds masturbation and self-abuse young boys need it special its all electric and very technical you sit down anywhere some sex wheel sidles up your ass or clamps onto your spine centers and the electronic gallows will just kill you on a conveyor belt the Director there bellowing orders:

"I want you to shit and piss all over yourself when you see the gallows. Synchronize your castor oil will you? And give the pitiless hang boy an imploring look for Chrisakes he's your ass hole buddy about to hang you and that's the *drama* of it . . ."

"It's a sick picture B.J."

Well it seems this rotten young prince gives off whiffs of decay when he moves but he doesn't move much as a rule has eyes for one of the prisoners wants him for his very own fish boy but the younger generators are on the way. Partisans have seized a wing of the studio and called in the Red Guards . . . "Now what do you boys *feel* about a situation like this? Well go on express yourselves . . This is a *progressive* school . . These youths of image and association now at entrance to the garden carrying banners of interlanguage . . Her fourth-grade class screamed in terror when I looked at the 'dogs' and I looked at the pavement decided the pavement was safer . . Attack enemy over instrument like pinball . . Shift tilt STOP the GOD film. Frame by frame take a good look boys . ."

"They got this awful mollusk eats the hanged boys body and soul in the orgasm and they love being eaten because of this liquefying gook it secretes and rubs all over them but maybe I'm talking too much about private things."

"You boys going to stand still for this? Being slobbered down and shit out by an alien mollusk? Join the army and see the world I remember this one patrol had been liberating a river town and picked up the Sex Skin habit. This Sex Skin is a critter found in the rivers here wraps all around you like a second skin eats you slow and good . . Well these boys had the Sex Skin burned off by the sun crossing the plain they could just crawl when they reached the post quivering sores they was half eaten mostly shit and pieces of them falling off so I called the captain and he said best thing was bash their skulls in and bury them in the privy where he hoped the smell might pass unnoticed but there was stink in congress about 'unsung heroes' and the President himself nailed a purple heart to that privy you can still see where the old privy used to be other side of those thistles there . .

"Now that should show you fellows something of the situation out here and the problems we have to face . . take the case of a young soldier who tried to rescue his buddy from a Sex Skin and it grew onto him and now his buddy turns from him in disgust . . anyone would you understand and that's not the worst of it it's knowing at any second your buddy may be took by the alien virus it's happened cruel idiot smile over the corn flakes . . You gasp and reach for a side arm looking after your own soul like a good Catholic . . too late . . your nerve centers are paralyzed by the dreaded Bor-Bor he has slipped into your Nescafé . . He's going to eat you slow and nasty . . This situation here has given rise to what the head shrinkers call 'ideas of persecution' among our personnel and a marked slump in morale . . As I write this I have barricaded myself in the ward room against the 2nd Lieutenant who claims he is 'God's little hang boy sent special to me' that fucking shave tail I can hear him out there whimpering and slobbering and the Colonel is jacking off in front of the window pointing to a Gemini Sex Skin. The Captain's corpse hangs naked at the flagpole. I am the only sane man left on the post. I know now when it is too late what we are up against: a biologic weapon that reduces healthy clean-minded men to abject slobbering inhuman things undoubtedly of virus origins. I have decided to kill myself rather than fall into their hands. I am sure the padre would approve if he knew how things are out here. Don't know how much longer I can hold out. oxygen reserves almost exhausted. I am reading a science fiction book called *The Ticket That Exploded*. The story is close enough to what is going on here so now and again I make myself believe this ward room is just a scene in an old book far away and long ago might as well be that for all the support I'm getting from Base Headquarters."

"You see the action, B.J.? All these patrols cut off light-years behind enemy lines trying to get through some fat-assed gum-chewing comic-reading Technical Sergeant to Base Headquarters and there is no Base Headquarters everything is coming apart like a rotten undervest . . but the show goes on . . love . . romance . . stories that rip your heart out and eat it . . Now how's this for an angle? Are you listening B.J.? This clean-living decent heavy metal kid and a cold glamorous agent from the Green Galaxy has been sent out to destroy him with a Sex Skin but she falls for the kid and she can't do it and she can't go back to her own people because of the unspeakable tortures meted out to those who fail on a Mission so they take off together in a Gemini space capsule perhaps to wander forever in trackless space or perhaps?"

winds
of time

The room was on the roof of a ruined warehouse swept by winds of time through the open window trailing grey veils of curtain sounds and ectoplasmic flakes of old newspapers and newsreels swirling over the smooth concrete floor and under the bare iron frame of the dusty bed — the mattress twisted and molded by absent tenants — ghost rectums, spectral masturbating afternoons reflected in the tarnished mirror — The boy who owned this room stood naked, remote mineral silence like a blue mist in his eyes — sound and image flakes swirled round him and dusted his metal skin with grey powder — The other green boy dropped his pants and moved in swirls of poisonous color vapor, breathing the alien medium through sensitive purple gills lined with erectile hairs pulsing telepathic communications — The head was smaller than the neck and tapered to a point — A silver globe floated in front of him — The two beings approached each other wary and tentative — The green boy's penis, which was the same purple color as his gills, rose and vibrated into the heavy metal substance of the other — The two beings twisted free of human coordinates rectums merging in a rusty swamp smell — spurts of semen fell through the blue twilight of the room like opal chips — The air was full of flicker ghosts who move with the speed of light through orgasms of the world — tentative beings taking form for a few seconds in copulations of light— Mineral silence through the two bodies stuck together in a smell of KY and rectal mucus fell apart in time currents swept back into human form — At first he could not remember — winds of time through curtain sounds — blue eyes blurred and twisted absent bodies — The blue metal boy naked now flooded back into his memory as the green boy-girl dropped spaceship controls in swirls of poisonous color — The blue boy reached out like an icy draught through the other apparatus — They twisted together paralyzed — He and Bradly grinding against each other in pressure seats, while heavy metal substance guided their ship through the sickening twist of human cloud

belts — galaxy X chartering a rusty swamp smell — Their
calculations went out in a smell of ozone — opal chip
neighborhood of the flicker ghosts who travel the far flung
edge of Galaxy X hover and land through orgasm —
flickering form of his companion naked in copulation space
suit that clung to his muscular blue silence — smell of
KY and rectal mucus in eddies of translucent green light
— his body flushed with spectral presences like fish of
brilliant colors flashing through clear water — tentative
beings that took form and color from the creatures skin
membrane of light — pulsing veins crosscrossed the two
bodies stuck together in slow motion time currents — lips
of tentative faces, rectums merging structure one body in
translucent green flesh —

Bradly's left arm went numb and the tingling paralysis
spread down his left side — He felt crushing weight of
the Green Octopus who was there to block any composite
being and maintain her flesh monopoly of birth and death
— Her idiot camp followers drew him into the Garden of
Delights — back into human flesh — The Garden of Delights is a vast tingling numbness surrounded by ovens of
white-hot metal lattice with sloped funnels like a fish trap
— Outside the oven funnels is a ruined area of sex booths,
Turkish baths and transient hotels — orgasm addicts
stacked in rubbish heaps like muttering burlap — phantom sex guides flashing dirty movies — sound of fear —
dark street life of a place forgotten — "It might take a
little while." The Garden of Delights . . GOD . . Remember my old C.O. standing there with a hangman's
noose in his hands . . "You see this noose, Lee? This
is a *weapon* . . an enemy *weapon*."

That was in 1962. In the years that followed I contacted a number of undergrounds with various aims methods and organizational setups among which was an equivocal group of assassins called the "White Hunters." Were they white supremacists or an anti-white movement far ahead of the Black Muslims? The extreme right or far left of the Chinese? Representatives of Hassan i Sabbah or the White Goddess? No one knew and in this uncertainty lay the particular terror they inspired. The District Supervisor received me in a paneled room with fireplace, a country house it would seem rain outside a misty landscape. After motioning me to a deep leather armchair the D.S. walked around behind me talking in a voice without accent or inflection, a voice that no one could connect to the speaker or recognize on hearing it again. The man who used that voice had no native language. He had learned the use of an alien tool. The words floated in the air behind him as he walked.

"In this organization, Mr Lee, we do not encourage togetherness, *esprit de corps*. We do not give our agents the impression of belonging. As you know most existing organizations stress such primitive reactions as unquestioning obedience. Their agents become addicted to orders. You will receive orders of course and in some cases you will be well-advised not to carry out the orders you receive. On the other hand your failure to obey certain orders could expose you to dangers of which you can have at this point in your training no conception. There are worse things than death Mr Lee for example to live under the conditions your enemies will endeavor to impose. And the members of all existing organizations are at some point your enemy. You will learn to know where this point is if you survive. You will receive your instructions in many ways. From books, street signs, films, in some cases from agents who purport to be and may actually be members of the organization. There is no certainty. Those who need certainty are of no interest to this department. This is in point of fact a *non-organization* the aim of which is to immunize our agents against fear despair and death. We intend to break the birth-death cycle. As you know inoculation is the weapon of choice against virus and inoculation can only be effected through exposure . . . exposure to the pleasures offered under enemy conditions: a computerized Garden of Delights: exposure to the pain posed as an alternative . . you remember the ovens I think . . exposure to despair: 'The end is the beginning born knowing' the unforgivable sin of despair. You attempted to be God that is to *intervene* and failed utterly . . . Exposure to death: sad shrinking face . . he had come a long way for something not exchanged born for something knowing not exchanged. He died during the night."

A series of oblique references: "Zurich Saturday morning meet the so convenient Webber family at the B.P. Auto Stop. Hear realize that B.P. is not only and you'll find them buying everything from organization Shannon believe they can tape recorded at 23 Mount St it is that's what I thought and there's a little boy that's been reproduced in a lot of books hasn't it? He has a plate camera is it going to be published in *Vogue*? Part of the city's Friday child loving Tuesday for that matter oh really St. Louis Encephalitis of birth and nickname that's the only time 19 have died but the disease quickly spread. What in

Germany? He had been meaning Sexexcellency Sally Rand cunning Navy pilot Alan B. Weld two acts for three saints in outer space proudly registered in Phoenix was it are you sure that's right infectious night biter Mo. 18 I'm going to answer the doorbell definitely definitely the first time in thirty years Houston's outbreak the first time in who said Atlantic City? I was supposed to have done the sets for it and B. was supposed to acquire the virus from birds yeah then I think they paid a dollar for infectious disease processing the actual film but the disease quietly spread to all West Texas beauty unscheduled in outer space . . 'You mean you did it yourself you didn't have your assistant do it?' . . 'Nope just spreading epidemic of St Vacine maybe we should' . . 'How long did it take you to process this photo to squirt at anything that flew dyeing and all that it's all part of the city's sudden healthy people infectious beauty disease spreading epidemic of immune humans . . Half an hour? St. Louis Mo. giving hope you mean it's not finished yet? This photo the stripper exuberance its going to fade away? You should have that have a page fading away Time September—(a number not clear)—It is a musical family . . parachute just in case . . I can now drink reservoirs of the disease is that a new play to get at the source spray everything? I heard Friday's child loving a registered stripper nicknamed Conny oh are you going to remember this later that last of the last ditches like you came through the door in his moon suit maybe he's there? Oh no . . It's getting too spooky I'm getting the spinal cord and brain a male with female laughter they have this script he just dropped it like that they always start hissing it's all part of the game of war infants pay the price female laughter just came out of Time Starlet Weld Tuesday what? That's beautiful that is fogged out in distance there should be somebody so called actually this is how the old saw 'I think sex is healthy' just two stoned Germans naturally did the same long shuffle . . That's the clock if you set it two hours in advance the last of the last like we are in London a sentence words together in and out you know Manic Goddess 18 of 19 was done the painting was done never look at a model uninhibited disease by us astonishing we had done it without ever having a model starlet trapped in the sentence with full stop young painter are models myself look have you been there already?"

Leafing through the GOD files . . Ref. The Big Survey page 71: "Monday May 9" chills light fever . . my brain feels like all the connections are burnt out . . electric sex prickles . . The Garden of Delights kinda run down now charred wooden beams blue and pink tinsel dirty pictures flapping in the wind smell of coal gas . . heavy darkness of underexposed film has settled in that gloomy valley . . The body of a hanged man the rope around his neck is laying across the trap of a wooden gallows . . Carl standing there . .

"You led me into this ambush?"

He laughed and threw himself back on a bunk tossing his legs in the air, "What and me so young and genial?" a male with female laughter.

I walked away from him in disgust. Two guards were there one named "Rose." "Rose" was the more communicative and friendly and I asked him about the hanged man I had seen. He shrugged . . "Thought he would learn something . . his pants . . the plague."

I had walked up a slight incline. The garden was built in a valley quite bare except for scrub and vines. The whole place presented the sordid and run-down appearance of an abandoned carnival.

"Who planned all this?" I asked

The other guard answered: "Maybe it was him," pointing to Carl. "He will show you his country card in the end and the end is you hang on Tuesday."

Furniture stacked up for storage or removal and I find an old Webley 455 revolver in a dusty desk drawer. Standing there with the gun in my hand and Carl laughed again. The first bullet smashed into a beam a quarter-inch from his neck. Wood splinters spattered the young cheek with red dots. He rubbed a hand across his face and looked at the blood. He stopped laughing and looked at me his mouth a little open. At the second shot a jet of black liquid from the gun hit him in the mouth. His face turned black and old and he sagged against the beam muttering: "sleeping pills."

"genial"? hummm an odd word to use . . Ah here we are . . ref. East Beach File page 156: "This is a novel presented in a series of oblique references . . shave? . . did he? . . an amputation . . three young burglars one wearing a black overcoat stopped on the stairs by two English detectives . . *One of the thieves is nicknamed Genial* . ."

I put through a call to Scotland yard . . "Inspector Murdock please."

"Who shall I say is calling sir?"

"Klinker."

"Just 'Klinker' sir?"

"That's all."

"Oh hello Lee what can I do for you?"

"Anybody in your files nicknamed 'Genial'?"

"Hold on I'll check . . ." I put in another six pence waiting. "Yes here we are . . name Terrence Weld . . age 20 . . 5 feet 11 inches . . ten stone . . hair sandy . . eyes green . . known M.P. . . arrested three times suspected of breaking and entering . . no convictions . . ."

"How did he get that nickname?"

"smooth talker . . cool . . laughs a lot . . well genial on the surface at least."

"I see . . anything else?"

"Well yes . . about two years ago a chap named Harrison John Harrison hanged himself in the barn of his country place near Sandhill . . Harrison was living with young Weld at the time . . Weld was picked up in Harrison's car . . That's how it came to our attention . . needless to say no charges . ."

"Needless to say . . Was Weld staying with Harrison in his country place at the time of Harrison's death?"

"No he was in London."

"Nothing to connect him with Harrison's death?"

"Nothing whatever."

"Anything unusual about Harrison's suicide?"

"Well yes . . He'd rigged up a gallows with a drop . . must have taken half an hour to build."

"Anything else?"

pause . . cough . . "The body was completely naked."

"You're sure he was alone at the time?"

"Quite sure . . It's a small town . . easy to check."

"And his clothes . . all in a heap?"

"Neatly folded."

"And the tools he used?"

"Each tool returned to its place . . the barn was used as a workshop . . Carpentry was one of Harrison's hobbies."

"Did Harrison own a tape recorder?"

"How should I know? If you're all that interested I can give you a number to call in the S.B."

"Seems odd they should be interested in a routine suicide."

"A lot of the things they do seem odd to the rest of us. I do know they spent some time on the case . . Ask for Extension 12 . . Mr Taylor."

I could tell by the way he repeated the name Mr Taylor knew who I was

"Yes Mr Lee?"

"I'd like some information about a man named Harrison who killed himself two years ago . . country place near Sandhill . ."

"I remember the case . . rather not talk over the phone . . Can you meet me this evening in the Chandoo Bar? around six?"

Mr Taylor was dressed in a light-blue suit the shoulders so broad as to give an impression of deformity . . little scar where a harelip had been corrected . . red face . . light-blue eyes. We found a quiet corner. Mr Taylor ordered a Scotch Old Fashioned.

"John Harrison was 28 at the time of his death . . He was fairly well off . . flat in Paddington . . country place . . interested in the occult . . wrote bad poetry . . . painted bad pictures . . good at carpentry though . . made his own furniture."

"Did he own a tape recorder?"

"Yes he owned three tape recorders arranged with extension leads so he could play or record from one to the other. They were in the Paddington flat."

"You heard his tapes?"

He drank half his drink. "Yes I heard his tapes and read his diary. He seems to have been obsessed with hanging .. the sexual aspects you understand."

"That is not so unusual .. when you consider the extensions .."

He finished his drink. "No it's not so unusual and that is precisely what concerns this department."

"Did you interview a young man named Terrence Weld in this connection?"

"Young 'Genial'? Yes I interviewed that specimen."

"He was genial?"

"Impeccably so. I considered him directly responsible for Harrison's death. When I told him so he said

" 'What and me so young?'

"Exactly. And then he laughed."

"Interesting sound."

"Very."

"You recorded it?"

"Of course."

"Rather stupid on his part wouldn't you say so?"

"Not stupid exactly. He simply doesn't think the way we do. Perhaps he can't help laughing like that even when it would seem to be very much to his disadvantage to do so."

"I would suggest that 'Genial' is that laugh .. only existence 'Genial' has."

"Infectious laughter what? Yes he's a disease .. a virus.

There have been other cases. We try to keep it out of the papers."

"And cases that no one hears about? Perhaps the operation has been brought to the point where actual hanging is no longer necessary . . death attributed to natural causes . . or the victim is taken over by the virus . . 'Genial' himself may well have been 'hanged'."

"I'd thought of that of course. What we are dealing with here is a biologic weapon used by what powers and for what precise purpose we don't know yet."

"Also an ideal weapon for individual assassinations. Any reason why anyone might have wanted Harrison out of the way?"

"None whatever. He simply was not important. I concluded that his death was purely experimental."

"Was 'Genial' paid off?"

"It would seem so. He went to America shortly after I talked with him."

"Still there?"

"No he's back in London."

"You've seen him?"

"Yes. He didn't recognize me . . on junk and barbiturates . . looks ten years older . . down for the count I'd say . . But any one 'Genial' isn't important plenty more where he came from: out of a tape recorder."

"You made copies of Harrison's tapes?"

"Yes. Play them for you if you like."

Taylor's flat was compact carpeted . . a desk a typewriter two filing cabinets a long table by the window with four tape recorders connected by extension leads He pointed to the recorders . . "I got the idea from Harrison's setup."

"Did Harrison install the recorders himself?"

"No he was good at carpentry but had a blind spot so far as machinery goes especially electrical equipment. 'Genial' wired the machines for him"

He put on a tape. "The voices of Harrison and 'Genial' alternated. They both recorded a short text then the two tapes were cut into short sections and spliced in together. This produces a strong erotic reaction. Curiously enough the content of the tape doesn't seem to effect the result. In fact the same sexual effect can be produced by splicing in street recordings recorded by two subjects separately."

two voices reading one cruel mocking the other muffled and broken by comparison alternated at short intervals conveyed a sensation of charged electric intimacy easy vulgar and therefore disgusting.

"Now listen to this." The words were smudged together. They snarled and whined and barked. It was as if the words themselves were called in question and forced to give up their hidden meanings. "Inched tape . . the same recording you just heard pulled back and forth across the head . . You can get the same effect by switching a recording on and off at very short intervals. Listen carefully and you will hear words that were not in the original text: 'do it-do it-do it . . yes I will will will do it do it do it . . really really really do it do it do it . . neck neck neck . . oh yes oh yes oh yes . .'

"You heard?"

"Oh yes oh yes oh yes" (I reflected it would be interesting to inch a speech in the U.N., Congress, Parliament, or wherever and play back a few seconds later. You can run a government without police if your conditioning program is tight enough but you can't run a government without bull shit.) "Yes I heard."

Here's another one from the same original tape alternating Harrison and 'Genial' 24 times per second. I suspect this was the tape that dropped Harrison."

A familiar sound I had heard it for years barely audible . . loud and clear now a muttering hypnotic cadence. He shut the machine off.

"The sound track *illuminates* the image . . 'Genial's' image in this case . . almost tactile . . Well there it is . . biologists talk about creating life in a test tube . . all they need is a few tape recorders: 'Genial 23' at your service sir . . a virus of course . . The sound track is the only existence it has no one hears him he is not there except as a potential like the spheres and crystals that show up under an electron microscope: Cold Sore . . Rabies . . Yellow Fever . . St. Louis Encephalitis . . just spheres and crystals until they find another host . . just an arrangement of iron molecules on a tape until 'Genial 23' takes another queen . . . of course parasitic life is the easiest form to create . . . I wonder if . . ."

"If one could make a good 'Genial'? I don't know. Experiments along this line are indicated . . ."

('You see the angle, B.J.? a *nice* virus . . beautiful symptoms . . a long trip combining the best features of junk hash LSD yage . . those who return have gained a radiant superhuman beauty . . !)

"Was 'Genial' staying in the Paddington flat at the time of Harrison's suicide?"

"No. He left Harrison a month before Harrison's death. Apparently Harrison offered him all the money he could raise to come back and live with him but 'Genial' refused. He was living with a young man. name was Cunningham . . Robert Cunningham . . splicing themselves in together . . so long as the spliced tape finds an outlet in actual sex contact it acts as an aphrodisiac . . nothing more . . But when a susceptible subject is spliced in with someone *who is not there* then it acts as a destructive virus . . the perfect murder weapon with a built-in alibi. 'Genial' was not there at the time. He never is."

" 'Genial' didn't work this out for himself."

"Hardly . . This is obviously one aspect of a big picture . . what looks like a carefully worked out blueprint for invasion of the planet . . Anyone who keeps his bloody eyes open doesn't need a Harly St psychiatrist to tell him that destructive elements enter into so-called normal sex relations: the desire to dominate, to kill, to take over and eat the partner . . these impulses are normally held in check by counter impulses . . what the virus puts out of action is the *regulatory centers in the nervous system* . . We know now how it is done at least this particular operation . . We don't know who is doing it or how to stop them. Everytime we catch up with someone like 'Genial' we capture a tape recorder . . usually with the tapes already wiped off . . ."

"You must have some idea."

"We do . . You know about the Logos group?? . . claim to have reduced human behavior to a predictable science controlled by the appropriate word combos. They have a system of therapy they call 'clearing.' You 'run' traumatic material which they call 'engrams' until it loses emotional connotation through repetition and is then refiled as neutral memory. When all the 'engrams' have been run and deactivated the subject becomes a 'clear' . . It would seem that a technique a tool is good or bad according to who uses it and for what purposes. This tool is especially liable to abuse. In many cases they become 'clear' by unloading their 'engram' tapes on somebody else. These 'engram' tapes are living organisms viruses in fact . . This does give a certain position of advantage . . any opposition crippled by 'engram' tapes . . the 'clears' burning with a pure cold flame of self-interest a glittering image that lights up clearer and clearer as it fragments other image and ingests the dismembered fragments . . Yes we know the front men and women in this organization but they are no more than that . . a façade . . tape recorders . . the operators are *not there* . ."

"Program empty body what?" I got up to leave. "Where can I find 'Genial'?"

"Boot's any midnight. You won't get anything out of him. He doesn't remember."

The guard was wearing a white life jacket — He led Bradly to a conical room with bare plaster walls — On the green mattress cover lay a human skin half inflated like a rubber toy with erect penis — There was a metal valve at base of the spine —

"First we must write the ticket," said the guard (Sound of liquid typewriters plopping into gelatine) —

The guard was helping him into skin pants that burned like erogenous acid — His skin hairs slipped into the skin hairs of the sheath with little tingling shocks — The guard molded the skin in place shaping thighs and back, tucking the skin along the divide line below his nose — He clicked the metal valve into Bradly's spine — Exquisite toothache pain shot through nerves and bones — His body burned as if lashed with stinging sex nettles — The guard moved around him with little chirps and giggles — He goosed the rectum trailing like an empty condom deep into Bradly's ass — The penis spurted again and again as the guard tucked the burning sex skin into the divide line and smoothed it down along the perineum, hairs crackling through erogenous purple flesh — His body glowed a translucent pink steaming off a musty smell —

"Skin like that very hot for three weeks and then —" the guard snickered — 'wearing the Happy Cloak . . Happy Cloak addicts lasted about two years on the average. The thing was a biological adaptation of an organism found in the Venusian seas. It had been illegally developed after its potentialities were first realized. In its native state it got its prey by touching it. After that neurocontact had been established the prey was quite satisfied to be ingested you remember they make happy cloaks from a submarine thing that subdues its prey through a neuro-contact and eats it alive—only the victim doesn't want to get away once it has sampled the pleasures of the cloak. It was a beautiful garment a living white like the white of a pearl, shivering softly with rippling lights, stirring with a terrible ecstatic movement of its own as the lethal symbiosis was established' . . quoted from *Fury* by Henry Kuttner Mayflower Dell paperbacks, Kingsbourne House, 229231 High Holborn, London W.C.1 . .

Bradly was in a delirium where any sex thought immediately took three-dimensional form through a maze of Turkish baths and sex cubicles fitted with hammocks and swings and mattresses vibrating to a shrill insect frequency that danced in nerves and teeth and bones — "a thin singing shrillness that touched the nerves as well as the ears and made them vibrate ecstatically to the same beat" . . quote from *Fury* by Henry Kuttner page 143. The sex phantoms of all his wet dreams and masturbating afternoons surrounded him licking kissing feeling — From time to time he drank a heavy sweet translucent fluid brought by the guard — The liquid left a burning metal taste in his mouth — His lips and tongue swelled perforated by erogenous silver sores — The skin glowed phosphorescent pink purple suffused by a cold menthol burn so sensitive he went into orgasm at a current of air while uncontrolled diarrhea exploded down his thighs — The guard collected all his sperm in a pulsing neon cylinder — Through transparent walls he could see hundreds of other prisoners in cubicles of a vast hive milked for semen by the white-coated guards —The sperm collected was passed to central bank — Sometimes the prisoners were allowed contact and stuck together melting and welding in sex positions of soft rubber — At the center of this pulsing translucent hive was a gallows where the prisoners were hanged after being milked for three weeks — He could see the terminal cases carried to the gallows, bodies wasted to transparent mummy flesh over soft phosphorescent bones — Necks broken by the weight of suspension and the soft bones spurted out in orgasm leaving a deflated skin collected by the guards to be used on the next shift of prisoners — Mind and body blurred with pleasure some part of his being was still talking to the switchblade concealed under his mattress, feeling for it with numb erogenous fingers — One night he slipped into a forgotten nightmare of his childhood — A large black poodle was standing by his bed — The dog dissolved in smoke and out of the smoke arose a dummy being five feet tall — The dummy had a thin delicate face of green wax and long yellow fingernails —

"Poo Poo," he screamed in terror trying desperately to reach his knife — but his motor centers were paralyzed — This had happened before — "i told you i would come back" — Poo Poo put a long yellow corpse fingernail on his forehead vaulted over his body and lay down beside him — He could move now and began clawing at the dummy — Poo Poo snickered and traced three long scratches on Bradly's neck —

"You're dead, Poo Poo! dead! dead! dead!" Bradly screamed trying to pull the dummy head off —

"Perhaps i am — And you are too unless you get out of here — i've come to warn you — Out of present time past the crab guards on dirty pictures? — There's a Chinese boy in the next cubicle and Iam is just down the hall — He's very technical you know — And use this — i'm going now" —

He faded out leaving a faint impression on the green mattress cover — The room was full of milky light — (Departed have left mixture of dawn and dream) — There was a little bamboo flute on the bed beside Bradly — He put it to his lips and heard Poo Poo speak from an old rag in one corner — "Not now — Later" —

He contacted the Chinese boy who had smuggled in a transistor radio — They made plans quickly and when the guard came with the heavy liquid turned on the metal static and stabbed the switchblade deep into insect nerve centers — The guard fell twisting and flipping white juice from his ruptured abdomen — Bradly picked up the guard's gun and released the other prisoners — Most of them were too far gone to move but others they revived with static and formed a division of combat troops — Bradly showed the guard's weapon to Iam —

"How do you work this fucker?" —

Iam examined the mechanism with long fingers precise as tooled metal — explained it was camera gun with telescopic lens equipped to take and project a moving picture vibrating the image at supersonic speed — He attached the radio to the camera gun so that the static synchronized with the vibrations — Bradly had the gun ready in his hand as they zigzagged out of the hive rushing the metal points of the ovens — Guard towers opened up with magnetic spirals and Bradly lost half his men before he could hit the central control tower and deactivate the mechanical gun turrets — (His troops had one advantage — All the guards and weapons of the enemy were operated by machine control and they had no actual fighters on the location) — Zigzagging he opened up with camera gun and static — Towers and ovens went up in a nitrous blast of burning film — A great rent tore the whole structure of the garden to the blue sky beyond — He put the flute to his lips and blue notes of Pan trickled down from the remote mountain village of his childhood — The prisoners heard the pipes and streamed out of the garden — The sperm tanks drained into streets of image forming thunderbolts of plasma that exploded The Garden of Delights in a flash of silver light — The Green Pine Inn is on a bluff over the river . . a lawn with chairs and tables stretches down to the edge of the bluff. The family is sitting on a screened porch fried chicken hot biscuits iced tea on the table. At one end of the table opposite his father is a boy about 18 dressed in a blue suit . . a slash of red on each cheekbone. He is looking across the valley.

The Demolition Squad has arrived. The G.O.D. is being pulled down and stacked into piles for burning. A lean leather-faced man with pale grey eyes looks sourly at a broken gallows covered with pink tinsel. A tape recorder gasps, shits, pisses, strangles and ejaculates at his feet. He listens his face impassive. He swings his heavy metal tipped boot. The noise stops. He leans forward and picks up a piece of twisted film streaked with excrement and holds it up to the late afternoon sun. He lets his arm drop and the film twists from his fingers. He glances around. "All set I guess."

Men step forward sloshing pails of gasoline. The foreman throws a match and steps back. Other fires are starting here and there across the valley the smoke hanging black and motionless in the still September air. The Demolition Squad is walking up the hill to their truck . . a clank of tools. The two garden guards, who have been waiting there for a lift to town, get in . . a grinding of gears . . sound of a distant motor. Behind them in a darkening valley the Garden of Delights is scattered piles of smoldering rubbish . . . scrub and vines grow through blackened tape recorders where goats graze and lizards bask in the afternoon sun. G.O.D. is the smell of burning leaves in cobblestone streets a rustle of darkness and wires frayed sounds of a distant city.

The Guard named Rose sitting on a bench in the back of a swaying truck with the silent demolition men. He does not know where he is going or what he will do when he gets there . . . "getting old . . watchman in a warehouse . . museum guard maybe . . "

I stopped at a newsstand on Shaftesbury Avenue and bought a copy of *Encounter* contemplating under Eros the feat of prose abstracted to a point where no image track occurs.

(The concomitance or rather juxtaposition with this relentlessly successful though diagrammatic schemata by sexualizing syntactically delinquent analogous metaphor)

It was 11:50 P.M. when I stepped into the entrance of Boot's and there was "Genial" standing outside blue neon on his face you thought of diseased metal when you looked at him a face burning in slow cold fires.

(desperately effete negation of societal values fecundate with orifices perspective and the ambivalent smugness of unavowed totalitarianism.)

I knew why he was standing there. He didn't have the ready to fill his script. He was waiting for somebody he could touch.

(foundering in disproportionate exasperation he doesn't even achieve the irrelevant honesty of hysteria but rather an uneasy somnolence counterpointed by the infantile exposure of fragmentary suburban genitalia.)

"Need bread for your script, man?"

He turned and looked at me decided I wasn't the heat

and nodded. I passed him a quid. "That should buy six jacks. I'll see you outside."

He nodded again went in and sat down in the script line.

(ironically the format is banal to its heart of pulp ambivalently flailing noneffectual tentacles of verbal diarrhea)

I waited half an hour of word sludge

(confirming the existence of their creator their periodically jolted lives starved of direction or vector by the recognizable official negative analogues banal "privatisation" being the most reliable)

"You can fix at my place if you like."

I could tell he had no place of his own. He just nodded and we got in a cab. I had to wake him up when we got there and help him up the stairs. He'd been hitting the goof balls waiting on his script. I deposited him in a chair. He slumped forward and his tongue lolled out. He opened one eye and looked at me.

"Don't I know you from some place?"

"Right back where we started from born knowing."

His eyes touched me inside. He smiled twisting a Sammy scarf in his dirty fingers.

"You should have let me finish the job instead of leaving it half done."

(species spawning for such a purpose to ask reputably informed complacent "What is it for?" Accessibility is I feel to beg the question.)

"I'm immune now remember."

"Yes thanks to me."

"Thanks 'Genial.'"

"So what did it get you?" He pointed to the mirror. "Look at you .. burnt out used up ..."

(to traduce or transfigure and reduce a man's pulsating multiplicity to untranslatable inchoate word for latent consensus of "otherness")

"And look at you 'Genial' . . . sex scar tissue on anyone I ever asked alive or dead I should know."

(Mr S. who latterly became something the point is simply the contradictions of an inherent territory prophet stridently inclined to gritty acceptances depending on banal illiterate process of perceptive engagement)

I found "Genial" in the police shed on top of the hill. He was sitting on a bench his face blank as an empty screen. A police sergeant behind a desk squinted through cigarette smoke. "Much trouble this one," he pointed to 'Genial,' "papers *muy malo no en ordenes . .*"

"He has a passport?"

"Oh yes but the date here and the date here *no corresponde . . muy malo . .* perhaps the passport is false .. it will have to be sent to the Capitol of course .."

He watched my hand and checked the denomination of the note I was slipping under the frayed green blotter.

He picked up the passport and leafed through it. "Oh yes .. here is the date of entry .. Yes everything quite in order .. your passport *señor . .*"

"Genial" stood there with the passport in his hand .. "Come along 'Genial.'" I put a hand under his arm and led him out onto the road.

"*Adiós señores.*"

"*Adiós.*"

I guided "Genial" with one hand under an elbow. He

weighed no more than his clothes. We sat down under a tree worn smooth by others who sat there before or after time switched the tracks through a field of little white flowers by the ruined signal tower. We remember the days as long procession of the secret police always everywhere in different form. outside Guayaquil sat on a river bank and saw a big lizard cross the mud flats dotted with melon rind thrown from passing canoes. It was the end of the line. My death across his face faded through the soccer scores the urinal and the bicycle races . . faded into Iam's face at the Green Inn looking across the valley.

He was standing on a Moroccan hillside with his troops and around them the Pan pipes calm and impersonal as the blue sky — From his pocket he heard Poo Poo say "Take me with you" — He felt a little plastic bag and drew it out — There was a flat grey membrane inside it — He moved away on Pan pipes to the remote mountain village of his childhood where blue mist swirled through the streets and time stopped in the slate houses — Words fell from his mind — He drifted through wind chimes of subway dawns and turnstiles — Boys on roller skates turned slow circles in a shower of ruined suburbs — grey luminous flakes falling softly on Ewyork, Aris, Ome, Oston — crumpled cloth bodies through the glass and metal streets swept by time winds — from siren towers the twanging tones of fear — positive feedback Pan God of Panic piping blue notes through empty streets as the berserk time machine twisted a tornado of centuries — wind through dusty offices and archives — board books scattered to rubbish heaps of the earth — symbol books of the all powerful board that had controlled thought feeling and movement of a planet with iron claws of pain and pleasure from birth to death — control symbols pounded to word and image dust; crumpled cloth bodies of the vast control machine — The whole structure of reality went up in silent explosions under the whining sirens — Pipers from his remote mountain villages loosed Pan God of Panic through streets of image — dead nitrous streets of an old film set — paper moon and muslin trees and in the black silver sky great rents as the cover of the world rained down in luminous film flakes — The 1920's careened through darkening cities in black Cadillacs spitting film bullets of accelerated time —

through the open window trailing swamp smells and old newspapers — orgasm addicts stacked in the attic like muttering burlap — the mattress molded on all sides masturbating afternoons reflected; "Difficult to get out" — word and image skin like a rubber toy dusted with grey spine powder — Blue notes of Pan trickled down silver train whistles — calling the imprisoned Jinn from copulation space suits that clung to his muscle lust and burning sex skin — The green fish boys dropped their torture of spectral presence and like fish left the garden through clear water — Tentative beings followed the music membrane of light and color — Pipes of Pan trickled down sleeping comrade of his childhood — pure blue jabs through the Garden of Delights — cutting the black insect — He slipped out of time in a — His camera gun blasted memory — The blue boy reached from the remote mountain village other apparatus — They twisted cool and impersonal as the sky against each other in pressure seats — stuck together in slow-motion faces —

crisscrossed with tentative whistles of other lips broken
now from birth to death — control skin melted leaving
crumpled cloth bodies of muttering burlap — Explosion
swept through empty sex thoughts as the sperm tanks
drained into streets of image — the cover of the world
rained down — all from an old movie will give at his
touch.

*in a
strange bed*

Lykin was the first to awake — He could not remember where he was — Slowly his blue eyes blurred
with exhaustion registered glowing red rocks and metallic
shrubs with silver leaves that surrounded the little pool
where he lay — The ghastly night flooded back into his
memory — Controls of their space craft had suddenly
blanked out by the intervention of an invisible alien force
like an icy draught through the cabin — Not only the
mechanical controls had been put out of action but their
nerve centers had been paralyzed — He and Bradly the
Co-pilot had sat helpless in their pressure seats for two
hours while the invading force guided their ship in a
sickening spiral through the poisonous cloud belts of an
unknown planet — Lykin and Bradly had blacked out
when they landed — How had they gotten out of the
ship? — He stood up and tripped over the sleeping form
of his companion naked except for the skin-tight transparent space suit that clung to his muscular body — He
decided to have a quick look at the terrain before waking

Bradly — He was at the bottom of a gully surrounded by red rocks of some translucent substance — He climbed out of the gully and found himself on a plateau — A fantastic landscape of multicolored rock carved like statues of molten blue lava interspaced with stalagmites of a pearly white intensity he had never experienced in his previous explorations — The sky was like a green ocean — There were four suns on the horizon around the plateau, each sun of a different color — Blue, green, red, and one (much larger than the others) a brilliant silver — The air was of a tingling clarity that seemed to support his body so that movements were incredibly precise and easily performed — He turned and started back down the gully toward the pool — He felt a click in his brain like a crystal flare and heard a silver voice: "Come stranger" — Bradly was accustomed to telepathic phenomena but this voice was unusually clear and immediate — He climbed over a large rock and saw the pool — His friend was still asleep — Beside him sat an amphibious green fish boy shimmering with water from the pool — The creature pulsed with translucent green light that flooded through the flesh in eddies — The head was a pointed dome that sprang from a slender neck on either side of which protruded gills like sensitive spongy wings — The creature was covered by a membranous substance with a network of transparent veins — The body surface was in constant motion like slow water dripping down a statue — The face was almost flat but with lips and nose sharply and beautifully delineated and huge liquid eyes above the high ridged cheekbones the delicate structure of which shone through transparent skin — The being was sitting in a cross-legged position and from its thighs jutted small silver fins of fine gauze — The slender sinuous legs ended in webbed flippers — Between the legs Lykin could see the genitals half aroused in curiosity as the fish boy stroked the head of his sleeping companion and touched the space suit with tentative jabs of its long green fingers — Lykin moved cautiously so as not to frighten the creature back into the pool — The fish boy turned and looked at him with a shy dreamy smile — An electric shiver ran up his spine and burst in crystal fish syllables: "Approach stranger — Have no fear" — The creature's mouth had not moved — Lykin moved forward with excitement tingling through his body and knelt beside the water boy who extended a dripping hand and lightly clasped his shoulder — A thrill ran through him from the contact — Underwater memory bubbles burst in his brain — He was in the alien medium, squirming in crystal rock pools and basking on edges of limestone fanned by giant ferns in the sound of dripping water — Swimming through ruined cities with the water creatures twisting in slow swirls of orgasm, shooting out explosions of colored bubbles to the surface, trailing blue streamers —

Ali woke in a strange bed to find the proprietor standing over him, "Who the fuck are you and what are you doing in my apartment?" Ali flashed back to the suburban cocktail party — music from the '20s — old women doing the Charleston — and the Irishman with iron-grey hair who looked like a con cop from vaudeville —

"Easy way and a tough way to do things, kid — i can put you up for the night in this apartment — The owner is out of town and i dont *think* he'll be back before tomorrow night — "

"But Mr O'Brien said — "

"Tell O'Brien he can stay in his own precinct — This happens to be my apartment — Put on your dry goods and cut — "

Ali dressed hastily — Tucking his shirt he slipped out into the American suburb — The streets were empty and clean like after a heavy rain — At an intersection of cracked concrete boys turned slow circles on roller skates under a half-moon in the morning sky, swept by storms of color as the sun rose — Ali felt his steps lighter and lighter — He floated away on eddies of blue and green — He alighted in the clear atmosphere of a green land where every blade of grass shone as if framed in crystal — The gravity pull was light so his feet barely touched the ground as he ran along clear streams of water under dripping trees — came to a city of worn marble streets and copper domes — In the lobby of a luxury hotel page boys in elaborate uniforms assessed his financial status with experienced eyes — On the wall was a little sign:

The Nature of Begging

Need ? —— Lack -

Want ? —— Need -

Life ? —— Death -

Ali walked out into the main square — fish smells and dead eyes in doorways — obscene gestures of proposition — In a dark side street off the square Ali found what looked like an old chemist's shop with jars of colored liquid in the window — A little black man, body bent by a fibrous tumor came forward to meet him with a chirp of interrogation — He was wearing double lens glasses that slid down on his nose — Ali drew out the plastic bag he carried with the flattened grey membrane inside — The shopkeeper took it in smooth black fingers and held it up to the light — He gave a little chirping call and his assistant came in from shadow recesses of the shop — It was some creature like a large grasshopper with a body that changed color as he walked past the jars — The eyes were crystal lens — His penis, which was held in upright position by a long silver cord extending into the abdomen, moved in flash erections to currents of color— He held the membrane in adzes and grafting tools that fitted into his fibrous finger stumps — As he looked his body pulsed a brilliant green — The shopkeeper nodded and brought out a jar about two feet high full of a heavy white fluid — The assistant opened the envelope with a little curved knife and dropped the membrane into the jar — As Ali watched the membrane stirred like a Japanese flower and blossomed into a tiny green newt with human head — The creature opened black liquid eyes for a few seconds then curled into foetal sleep and sank to the bottom of the jar — The shopkeeper covered the jar with a cloth and put it on a dark shelf — He smiled and drew a map on the counter — Starting from the shop a dotted line led to a system of canals, a pump, two penises in orgasm, closed eyes of sleep five times — Then the dotted line led back to the shop — He looked at Ali to be sure he understood — Ali nodded and walked on the dotted line — The marble streets ended in mud — He could see a system of canals with thatched huts and gardens and tanks tended by little black men with fibrous tumors and moles from which sprouted green hairs — They looked up from their work and flashed quick smiles —A heavy smell of compost heaps and rotten ponds filled the air — As he passed over a bridge a green newt boy surfaced in a canal smiled and masturbated quickly ejaculating an iridescent fluid that glinted in the clear light — He twisted with a mocking laugh and dove out of sight in the black water — Ali walked along the canal and found himself in a maze of pumps and locks and could not find how he got there or the way out — At the bottom of this maze a man in green tattered uniform motioned him to come down pointing to an iron stairway that led out on a wooden ramp — The man stood waiting at the end of the ramp — Ali walked toward him smiling like a dog — "i am a stranger here — i am sorry if — i do not know your laws" — The guard was smiling too — a slow familiar smile like: "Perhaps you don't go into the prison if" — flashed back to customs shed in South America — Ali bent over a chair feeling quick pants of the young policeman on his naked back — The carbine leaning against one wall sharp and clear in the flash bulb of orgasm — "So" — he thought "things are not different here" —

The man led him to a shed — Inside was a pallet on the floor — Clothing hung from wooden pegs — In another room he could see levers and wheels obviously controlling the pumps and locks — The man flicked Ali's clothes — He undressed slowly dropping his pants with a wriggling motion as his cock flipped out and up — The man stood naked in green light that filtered into the shed from overhanging vines and fruit trees — He picked Ali up in his arms and kissed him — His breath had a vegetable smell slightly rotten like tropical fruit — He carried Ali to the pallet and shoved his knees up to his ears — From a shelf he took a little jar of what looked like frogs' eggs and gave off an odor of moldy proteins — He rubbed the eggs into Ali's ass — Ali could feel something coming alive in his rectum and wriggling down into his testicles — The man slid his cock in — Ali squirmed teeth bared wriggling feelers caressing his penis rubbing around nerves at the tip — The man caught his ejaculation in the jar — Tiny green frogs with sucker paws stirred in the sperm —

He stayed for five nights with the man sleeping on the pallet and eating meals of fruit from the garden and helping with the wheels and levers — At the end of five days the man gave him the jar of eggs and he went back to the shop and gave the eggs to the shopkeeper —

The shopkeeper smiled and took the other jar down from the shelf — The green newt boy, still curled in sleep, had grown until it filled the jar — The shopkeeper drew a map on the counter dotted line to a hut in the canal system — And Ali walked out carrying the jar along the line to a hut where an old man greeted him — Ali uncovered the jar — The man clapped his hands softly and made a little clucking noise — He showed Ali a series of tanks behind his hut like an elaborate cesspool, one tank draining into another — In the tanks were green newt boys in various stages and the last tank opened out into black water of the canal — The man emptied the jar into the first tank — Ali turned to walk away and felt the man's hand on his shoulder, led him back into the hut — He measured Ali's neck like a tailor and selected from a shelf two dried gills which he fitted carefully and gave to

Ali in a plastic envelope — He motioned to the sky — He made a choking sound and pointed to the bag —

Ali began hustling around the square where the nobles cruised in the evening — dark street life of a place forgotten — The city was swept by waves of giant carnivorous land crabs and Ali learned to hide himself when he heard their snapping claws like radio static — Explosions of time film was another danger in the city — One evening in the square he heard a rumble like muffled thunder — Everyone running for the canals and shouting "The Studio went up" — A cloud of red nitrous fumes settled on the city — Ali, gasping and choking, remembered and reached for his plastic bag — He put the gills around his neck and dove into a wellhead carved to resemble a stone rectum — As he fell deep into the green water he could feel the gills cut into his neck — A sudden sharp taste of blood and he was breathing and swimming along an underground passage — He could see light ahead and came out into one of the open canals —

Ali woke in a strange bed — As you listen fill in with him "Who the fuck are you and what are you doing in my image track?" Ali was wide awake now and clicked "out of here," female impersonators, music back to the '20s, suburban pool halls and vaudeville voice of a grey-haired Irishman who turned over a steady stream of "easy way and a tough way to do time" — Meanwhile i had forgotten the owner in this apartment — scent of memory pictures — people gone — back tomorrow night —

"But Mr O'Brien said" —

"Tell O'Brien to stay in his own precinct — This happens to be my dawn wind in other flesh" —

Ali dressed hastily and slipped out — Board members, look, the streets are empty — Young faces melted the law, turned slow circles on roller skates — Nova Police look at the wired color sunrise — Errand boy floating on eddies of red and green alighted in slow-motion flashes of clear atmosphere — The gravity pull was lighter — does not know the frequency of junk — marble streets and copper domes — Darkened eyes of page boys in elaborate physical skin put his financial status out in the streets — East St. Louis music on chirping call — His genitals were voices out into other dressing rooms — long silver thread that extended in flash erections back and forth — switch to office of a garage — sharp desire held the membrane —

"Yes you have grafting tools — Without you i on pavement" —

The shopkeeper nodded good bye — translucent white fade-out — Sticky office spattered light on naked knives — from his face newsreels of riots moving in fast — Ali round the Board —

"What's this Japanese flower blossomed into sinking ship? You trying source of human head on screen?"

Boneless mummy curled into foetal tank — The shopkeeper covered — fade-out at dawn — Hurry up — Hands put it on a dark shelf — He smile and twist brain — starting with the shop a dotted corpse last round — the gate from two cocks in orgasm — men smoking on the end of the line — sleep five times — then the dotted line —

"We been subliminated in doorways," looked at Ali to be sure he understood, "Beside you wind voices on dotted line trailed system of canals — not think the Doctor on stage" —

They looked up from their work — empty all hate faces — vapor trails writing the sky — Some boy surfaced in the canal — Iridescent harbor glinted in the stellar light — mocking laugh of absent tenants — ghost riots along the canal and found himself in a garage — Stood naked — good bye of hydraulic pumps spattered on his face — out at the bottom interrogate substance of green uniform was motioning "want it" — tentative empty flesh of KY and rectal mucus? — End of the ramp man stood waiting — gate from human form — "We been subliminated like a dog — stranger face sucked in other apparatus" — "sorry if" —

The man was smiling, flapping vapor like rusty swamp smell — flicker back to a custom shed in South America — ("First we must write the ticket") — Feeling the quick pants of mummy — goosed his ass — carbine leaning against one wall — burning orgasm — wind voices beside masturbating pallet on the floor —

"Out of here, female impersonators" —

Wooden pegs in another room forgotten memory controlling the structure of his Scandinavian outhouse skin — The man flicked Ali's clothes — Prisoner pants with wriggling movement stood naked now in green mummy flesh, hanging vines and deflated skin — Death kissed him — His breath talked to the switchblade — He dropped Ali on the last parasite from the shelf before newsreels shut off — Looked like frog eggs — He was shoving the eggs — Poo Poo snickered, coming alive in his rectum like green neon — Into the prostate his slow fingers — Ali squirmed his teeth bared — The man caught his spurts like a pack of cards — He stayed for five nights in the tarnished office eating meals of fruit from color vapor — At the end of five days newsreels of riot move in fast — The eggs went back to boneless mummy — Ghost keeper smiled and fade-out at dawn — Hands of light fell apart in corpse — last jar — The shopkeeper drew a map in absent bodies — empty the canal area — Ali twisted through open shirt — He found his way to their ship in the harbor — The man travel on newsreels — Exquisite screen penis spurted again — corpse tanks — end of the line and last jar — led the Doctor on stage — Sex phantoms emptied the jars into afternoon image track — He turned to walk away and suffused the hut — people gone — Diarrhea exploded down from a shelf —

"Ali hanged after being milked, see?" made a choking noise and pointed — orgasm of a place forgotten — Corpses hang from gallows — "Land crabs" — He dissolved in smoke and crumpled cloth —

"All right, Doctor — Indications enough — i told you i would come — healed scars — The Studio went up — a cloud of nitrous Big Fix" — Ali gasped and choked and reached courage to pass without doing pictures around his neck — He could feel suddenly shut-off taste of blood and all the Garden of Delights — He could see sex scenes in the open canals of time —

*do you
love me?*

The young monk led Bradly to a cubicle — On a stone table was a tape recorder — The monk switched on the recorder and sounds of lovemaking filled the room — The monk took off his robe and stood naked with an erection — He danced around the table caressing a shadowy figure out of the air above the recorder — A tentative shape flickering in and out of focus to the sound track — The figure floated free of the recorder and followed the monk to a pallet on the floor — He went through a pantomime of pleading with the phantom who sat on the bed with legs crossed and arms folded — Finally the phantom nodded reluctant consent and the monk twisted through a parody of lovemaking as the tape speeded up: "Oh darling i love you oh oh deeper oh oh fuck the shit out of me oh darling do it again" — Bradly rolled on the floor, a vibrating air hammer of laughter shaking flesh from the bones — Scalding urine spurted from his penis — The Other Half swirled in the air above him screaming, face contorted in suffocation as he laughed the sex words from throat gristle in bloody crystal blobs — His bones were shaking, vibrated to neon — Waves of laughter through his rectum and prostate and testicles giggling out spurts of semen as he rolled with his knees up to his chin —

All the tunes and sound effects of *"Love"* spit from the recorder permutating sex whine of a sick picture planet: Do you love me? — But i exploded in cosmic laughter — Old acquaintance be forgot? — Oh darling, just a photograph? — Mary i love you i do do you know i love you through? — On my knees i hoped you'd love me too — I would run till i feel the thrill of long ago — Now my inspiration but it won't last and we'll be just a photograph — i've forgotten you then? i can't sleep, Blue Eyes, if i don't have you — Do i love her? i love you i love you many splendored thing — Can't even eat — Jelly on my mind back home — 'Twas good bye deep in the true love — We'll never meet again, darling, in my fashion — Yes eyes ever shining that made me my way — Always it's a long trip to Tipperary — Tell Laura i love my blue heaven — Get up woman up off your big fat earth out into cosmic space with all your diamond rings — Do you do you do you love me? — Lovey lovey dovey brought to mind? What? Do you love me with a banjo? — Please don't be angry — i wonder who — If i had learned to love you every time i felt blue — But someone took you out of the stardust of the skies — Your charms travel to remind me of you — together again — forgotten you eat — Don't know how i'll make it baby — blue eyes the color of — Do you love me? Love is *para olvidar* — Tell Laura oh jelly love you — i can't — Got you under my skin on my mind — But i'll always be true to my blue heaven — Love Mary? — Fuck the shit out of me — Get up off your big fat rusty-dusty — It's a long way to go, St. Louis woman — prospect of red mesas out to space — Do you love me? — Do you love void and scenic railways back home?? And do you love me with a banjo permutated through do you love me? — i wonder who permutated the structure every time i felt blue — But that was ferris wheels clicking in the stardust of the sky — on perilous tracks — i had a dog his name was Bill aworking clouds of *Me* — Tearing his insides apart — Need a helping hand? — understanding out of date — Find someone else at this time of day? Torch cutting through the eats? —

Don't know how i'll make it, baby — Electric fingers removed "*Love*" — Do you love me? — Love is red sheets of pain hung oh oh baby oh jelly — The guide slipped off his jelly — I've got you under my skin pulsing red light — Clouds of *Me* always be true to you — Hula hoops of color formed always be true to you darling in my Bradly — Weak and torn i'll hurry to my blue heaven as i sank in suffocation panic of rusty St. Louis woman — With just a photograph, Mary, you know i love you through sperm — Contraction turnstile hoped you'd love me too — Orgasm floated arms still i feel the thrill of slow movement but it won't last — i've forgotten you then? — i love you i love you and bones tearing his insides apart for the ants to eat — Jelly jelly jelly shifting color orgasm back home — Scratching shower of sperm that made cover of the board books — It's a long way to Tipperary — soft luminous spurts to my blue heaven — Pieces of cloud drifted through all the tunes from blue — Exploded in cosmic laughter of cable cars . . . Me? — Oh, darling, i love you in constant motion — i love you i do — You led Bradly into a cubicle on my knees — love floating in a slow vertigo of you — perilous tracks where wind whistled long ago — i can't sleep, baby, skin pulling loose if i don't have you — a peg like many splendored thing — i've got you deep in the guides body enclosed darling in *my* fashion — yes cool hands on his naked flesh my way — evening intestines of the other — Tell Laura i love her sucked through pearly genital woman off your big fat shower of sperm — Diamond rings spurt out of you — Should be brought to mind — Ejaculated bodies without a cover —

I learned to love you, pale adolescents — Someone took you out of the creature charms — We'll travel weak and torn by pain together — Silver films in the blood *para olvidar* — Tell Laura black fish movement of food love you — i can't sleep reflected in obsidian penis — Follow the swallow and released dream flesh in Isle of Capri — The truth in sunlight, Mary — memory riding the wind — It's a long way to go — someone walking — mountain wind —

Do i love you? — Crumpled cloth body ahoy — But remember the red open shirt flapping wind from you so true — Do you love me? — Vapor trails writing all the things you are — The great wind revolving what you could have — Indications in the harbor muttering blackbird — bye bye — Who's sorry now? — This time of day vultures in the street — 'Twas good bye on vacant lots — weeds growing through broken road — smell of healed and half-healed scars — all the little things you used to do on a bicycle built for little time so i'll say: "You on sidewalk" — if you were the only girl in green neon, your voices muttering in the dog rotation — Dollar baby, how cute can you be in desolate underbrush? You were meant for me? battered phonograph talk-face — I'm just a vagabond pass without — Can play the game as well as you, darling — train whistle open shirt flapping the cat and the fiddle — i am biologic from a long way to go — Nights are long with the St. Louis suburb — Music seems to whisper Louise Mary on the pissoirs — i had a dog his name was Bill — (In other flesh open shirt flapping) on the railroad — He went away — Many names murmur — Someone walking — won't be two — i'm half crazy all for the love of *"Good Night"* — Shadow voices belong to me — Found a million acoustic qualities couldn't reach in a five-and-ten-cent store — Naked boy on association line but you'll find someone else this time of day —

The levanto dances who's sorry now? — Hy diddle diddle the cat and the fiddle — Long way to Tipperary — fading khaki pants — Since you went away i see that moon hit the road into space — Do you love me Waltzing Matilda rock around railroad back home? lovey lovey dovey St. Louis Woman after hours — Do you love me with a banjo permutated Dead Man Blues? — If you don't i wonder who permutated the structure — Everybody love my baby — Lover man, that was ferris wheels clicking in a loverly bunch — solitude through the cables — turkey in the straw —

"BAR MAID WATCH THE EATS!!" —

Don't Know how i'll make it — one meat ball — Pull my daisy ding-dong love — Do you love me, love sheets? — Everybody's gonna have religion oh baby oh jelly — The guide slipped Paul under my skin pulsing red light — pallet on the floor darling Bradly — weak and torn sank in bones and shit of rusty St. Louis woman — when the saints go marching through all the popular tunes waiting for the sunrise in cosmic laughter of cable cars — the Sheik of Araby in constant motion — Blue moon — Margie — ice cream on my knees — Love floating in perilous tracks —

Do you love me, Nancy of the laughing sex words? — Still i feel the thrill of your charms vibrated to neon — giggling out all the little things you used to do — 'Twas good bye on the line of Bradly's naked body — love skin on a bicycle built for two — like a deflated balloon — Your cool hands on his naked dollars, baby — You were meant for me sucked through pearly genital face — Still i feel the thrill of you spurting out through the orgasm seems to whisper: "Louise, Mary, swamp mud" — In the blood little things you used to do — recorder jack-off — Substitute mine — Bye Bye body halves — i'm half crazy all for the love of color circuits — Do i love you in throat gristle? Ship ahoy but remember the red river body explode sex words to color — Do you love me? — Take a simple tape from all the things you are — Moanin' low my sweet 8276 all the time — Who's sorry now in the underwater street? 'Twas good bye on color bicycle built for response in the other nervous system —

I'm just a vagabond of the board books — written in can play the game as well as you — (That is color written the two compete) — Do i love you? i wonder — loose? if i don't have to? a peg like every time i felt blue? It's a long way through channels — Who's sorry now? chartered that memory street — Bye Bye — bodies empty — ash from falling tracks — Sweet man is going to go — Keep raining the throat designed to water — Remember every little thing you used to do — fish smell and dead — Know the answer? vacant lot the world and i were the only boy — jelly jelly in the stardust of the sky — i've got you deep inside of me enclosed darling in my fashion — Yes, baby, electric fingers removed flesh my way — Sheets of pain hung oh baby oh i love her sucked through pearly jelly — i've got you under big fat scratching clouds of me — Always be true to your diamond rings — Tell Laura black slow movement but it won't last — i've forgotten you then? Decay breathing? Black lust tearing his insides apart for ants? Love Mary? — The rose of memory shifting color orgasms back home — Good bye — It's a long way to go — Someone walking — Won't be two —

operation
rewrite

The "Other Half" is the word. The "Other Half" is an organism. Word is an organism. The presence of the "Other Half" a separate organism attached to your nervous system on an air line of words can now be demonstrated experimentally. One of the most common "hallucinations" of subjects during sense withdrawal is the feeling of another body sprawled through the subject's body at an angle . . yes quite an angle it is the "Other Half" worked quite some years on a symbiotic basis. From symbiosis to parasitism is a short step. The word is now a virus. The flu virus may once have been a healthy lung cell. It is now a parasitic organism that invades and damages the lungs. The word may once have been a healthy neural cell. It is now a parasitic organism that invades and damages the central nervous system. Modern man has lost the option of silence. Try halting your sub-vocal speech. Try to achieve even ten seconds of inner silence. You will encounter a resisting organism that *forces you to talk.* That organism is the word. In the beginning was the word. In the beginning of what exactly? The earliest artifacts date back about ten thousand years give a little take a little and "recorded"—(or prerecorded) history about seven thousand years. The human race is said to have been on set for 500,000 years. That leaves 490,000 years unaccounted for. Modern man has advanced from the stone ax to nuclear weapons in ten thousand years. This may well have happened before. Mr Brion Gysin suggests that a nuclear disaster in what is now the Gobi desert wiped out all traces of a civilization that made such a disaster possible. Perhaps their nuclear weapons did not operate on the same principle as the ones we have now. Perhaps they had no contact with the word organism. Perhaps the word itself is recent about ten thousand years old. What we call history is the history of the word. In the beginning of *that* history was the word.

The realization that something as familiar to you as the movement of your intestines the sound of your breathing the beating of your heart is also alien and hostile does make one feel a bit insecure at first. Remember that you can separate yourself from the "Other Half" from the word. The word is spliced in with the sound of your intestines and breathing with the beating of your heart. The first step is to record the sounds of your body and start splicing them in yourself. Splice in your body sounds with the body sounds of your best friend and see how familiar he gets. Splice your body sounds in with air hammers. Blast jolt vibrate the "Other Half" right out into the street. Splice your body sounds in with anybody or anything. Start a tapeworm club and exchange body sound tapes.

Feel right out into your nabor's intestines and help him digest his food. *Communication must become total and conscious before we can stop it.*

"The Venusian invasion was known as 'Operation Other Half,' that is, a parasitic invasion of the sexual area taking advantage, as all invasion plans must, of an already existing fucked-up situation ('My God what a mess.' The District Supervisor reminded himself that it was forbidden not only to express contempt for the natives but even to entertain such feelings. Bulletin 2323 is quite explicit on this point. Still he was unable to expunge a residual distaste for protoplasmic life deriving no doubt from his mineral origins. His mission was educational . . . the natives were to be scanned out of patterns laid down by the infamous 5th Colonists. Soon after his arrival he decided that he was confronting not only an outrageous case of colonial mismanagement but attempted nova as well. Reluctantly he called in the Nova Police. The Mission still functioned in a state of siege. Armed with nuclear weapons the 5th Colonists were determined to resist alterations. It had been necessary to issue weapons to his personnel. There were of course incidents . . casualties . . . A young clerk in the Cultural Department declared himself the Angel of Death and had to be removed to a rest home. The D.S. was contemplating the risky expedient of a 'miracle' and the miracle he contemplated was *silence.* Few things are worse than a 'miracle' that doesn't come off. He had of course put in an application to the Home Office underlining the urgency of his case contingent on the lengths to which the desperate 5th Colonists might reasonably be expected to go. Higher command had been vague and distant. He had no definite assurance that the necessary equipment would arrive in time. Would he have 3D in time?) — The human organism is literally consisting of two halves from the beginning word and all human sex is this unsanitary arrangement whereby two entities attempt to occupy the same three-dimensional coordinate points giving rise to the sordid latrine brawls which have characterized a planet based on 'the Word,' that is, on separate flesh engaged in endless sexual conflict — The Venusian Boy-Girls under Johnny Yen took over the Other Half, imposing a sexual blockade on the planet — (It will be readily understandable that a program of systematic frustration was necessary in order to sell this crock of sewage as Immortality, the Garden of Delights, and *love* —

"When the Board of Health intervened with inflexible authority, 'Operation Other Half' was referred to the Rewrite Department where the original engineering flaw of course came to light and the Venusian invasion was seen to be an inevitable correlate of the separation flesh gimmick — At this point a tremendous scream went up from the Venusians agitating to retain the flesh gimmick in some form — They were all terminal flesh addicts of course, motivated by pornographic torture films, and the entire Rewrite and Blueprint Departments were that disgusted ready to pull the switch out of hand to 'It Never Happened' — 'Unless these jokers stay out of the Rewrite room' —

"The Other Half was only one aspect of Operation Rewrite — Heavy metal addicts picketed the Rewrite Office, exploding in protest — Control addicts prowled the streets trying to influence waiters, lavatory attendants, *clochards,* and were to be seen on every corner of the city hypnotizing chickens — A few rich control addicts were able to surround themselves with latahs and sat on the terraces of expensive cafés with remote cruel smiles unaware i wrote last cigarette —

"My God what a mess — Just keep all these jokers out of the Rewrite Room is all" —

So let us start with one average, stupid, representative case: Johnny Yen the Other Half, errand boy from the death trauma — Now look i'm going to say it and i'm going to say it slow — Death *is* orgasm *is* rebirth *is* death in orgasm *is* their unsanitary Venusian gimmick *is* the whole birth death cycle of action — You got it? — Now do you understand who Johnny Yen is? The Boy-Girl Other Half strip tease God of sexual frustration — Errand boy from the death trauma — His immortality depends on the mortality of others — The same is true of *all* addicts — Mr Martin, for example, is a heavy metal addict — His life line is the human junky — The life line of control addicts is the control word — That is these so-called Gods can only live without three-dimensional coordinate points by forcing three-dimensional bodies on others — Their existence is pure vampirism — They are utterly unfit to be officers — Either they accept a rewrite job or they are all broken down to lavatory attendants, irrevocably committed to the toilet —

All right, back to the case of Johnny Yen — one of many such errand boys — Green Boy-Girls from the terminal sewers of Venus — So write back to the streets, Johnny, back to Ali God of Street Boys and Hustlers —

Write out of the sewers of Venus to neon streets of Saturn — Alternatively Johnny Yen can be written back to a green fish boy — There are always alternative solutions — Nothing is true — Everything is permitted —

    "No hassan i sabbah — we want flesh — we want junk — we want power —"

    "That did it — Dial *police*" —

the
nova police

    Bulletin from Rewrite: We had to call in the nova police to keep all these jokers out of the Rewrite Room — Can't be expected to work under such conditions — Introducing Inspector J. Lee of the nova police — "i doubt if any of you on this copy planet have ever seen a nova criminal — (they take considerable pains to mask their operations) and i am sure none of you have ever seen a nova police officer — When disorder on any planet reaches a certain point the regulating instance scans *police* — otherwise — Sput — Another planet bites the cosmic dust — i will now explain something of the mechanisms and techniques of nova which are always deliberately manipulated — i am quite well aware that no one on any planet likes to see a police officer so let me emphasize in passing that the nova police have no intention of remaining after their work is done — That is, when the danger of nova is removed from this planet we will move on to other assignments — We do our work and go —

    "The basic nova technique is very simple: Always

create as many insoluble conflicts as possible and always aggravate existing conflicts — This is done by dumping on the same planet life forms with incompatible conditions of existence — There is of course nothing 'wrong' about any given life form since 'wrong' only has reference to conflicts with other life forms — The point is these life forms should not be on the same planet — Their conditions of life are basically incompatible in present time form and it is precisely the work of the nova mob to see that they remain in present time form, to create and aggravate the conflicts that lead to the explosion of a planet, that is to nova — At any given time recorders fix the nature of absolute need and dictate the use of total weapons — Like this: Take two opposed pressure groups — Record the most violent and threatening statements of group one with regard to group two and play back to group two — Record the answer and take it back to group one — back and forth between opposed pressure groups — This process is known as 'feedback' — You can see it operating in any bar room quarrel — In any quarrel for that matter — Manipulated on a global scale feeds back nuclear war and nova — These conflicts are deliberately created and aggravated by nova criminals — The Nova Mob: 'Sammy the Butcher,' 'Green Tony,' 'the Brown Artist,' 'Jacky Blue Note,' 'Limestone John,' 'Izzy the Push,' 'Hamburger Mary,' 'Paddy The Sting,' 'the Subliminal Kid,' 'the Blue Dinosaur,' 'Willy the Rat' (who informed on his associates) and Mr and Mrs D also known as 'Mr Bradly Mr Martin' also known as 'the Ugly Spirit,' thought to be the leader of the mob — the nova mob — In all my experience as a police officer i have never seen such total fear and degradation on any planet — We intend to arrest these criminals and turn them over to the Biological Department for the indicated alterations —

"Now you may well ask whether we can straighten out this mess to the satisfaction of any life forms involved and my answer is this — Your earth case must be processed by the Biological Courts — (admittedly in a deplorable condition at this time) — No sooner set up than immediately corrupted so that they convene every day in a different location like floating dice games, constantly swept away by stampeding forms all idiotically glorifying their stupid ways of life — most of them quite unworkable of course) — attempting to seduce the judges into Venusian sex practices, drug the court officials, and intimidate the entire audience chamber with the threat of nova — In all my experience as a police officer I have never seen such total fear of the indicated alterations on any planet — a thankless job you see and we only do it so it won't have to be done some place else under even more difficult circumstances —

"The success of the nova mob depended on a blockade of the planet that allowed them to operate with impunity — This blockade was broken by partisan activity directed from the planet Saturn that cut the control lines of word and image laid down by the nova mob — So we moved in our agents and started to work keeping always in close touch with partisans — The selection of local personnel posed a most difficult problem — Frankly we found that most existing police agencies were hopelessly corrupt — The nova mob had seen to that — Paradoxically some of our best agents were recruited from the ranks of those

who are called criminals on this planet — In many in-
stances we had to use agents inexperienced in police work
— These were of course casualties and fuck-ups — You
must understand that an undercover agent witnesses the
most execrable cruelties while he waits helpless to intervene, sometimes for many years, before he can make a
definitive arrest — So it is no wonder that green officers
occasionally slip control when they finally do move in for
the arrest — This condition, known as 'arrest fever,' can
upset an entire operation — In one recent case, our man
in Tangier suffered an attack of 'arrest fever' and de-
tained everyone on his view screen including some of our
undercover men — He was transferred to paper work in
another area — Let me explain *how* we make an arrest —
nova criminals are not three-dimensional organisms —
(though they are quite definite organisms as we shall see)
— but they need three-dimensional human agents to
operate — The point at which the criminal controller
intersects a three-dimensional human agent is known as
'a coordinate point' — And if there is one thing that car-
ries over from one human host to another and established
identity of the controller it is *habit:* idiosyncracies, vices,
food preferences — (we were able to trace Hamburger
Mary through her fondness for peanut butter) — a gesture, a special look, that is to say the *style* of the controller — A chain smoker will always operate through
chain smokers, an addict through addicts — Now a single
controller can operate through thousands of human
agents, but he must have a line of coordinate points —
Some move on junk lines through addicts of the earth,
others move on lines of certain sexual practices and so

forth — It is only when we can block the controller out of all coordinate points available to him and flush him out from host cover that we can make a definitive arrest — Otherwise the criminal escapes to other coordinate" —

Question: "Inspector Lee, i don't quite understand what is meant by a 'coordinate point' — Could you make that a little clearer? —"

Answer: "Certainly — You see these criminal controllers occupy human bodies — ghosts? phantoms? Not at all — very definite organisms indeed — True you can't see them — Can you see a virus? — Well, the criminal controllers operate in very much the same manner as a virus — Now a virus in order to invade, damage and occupy the human organism must have a gimmick to get in — Once in the virus invades damages and occupies a certain area or organ in the body — known as the tissue of predilection — Hepatitis, for example, attacks the liver — Influenza the respiratory tract — Polio and rabies the central nervous system — In the same way a controller invades, damages and occupies some pattern or configuration of the human organism" —

Question: "How do these controllers gain access to the human organism?"

Answer: "I will give an example: the controllers who operate through addiction to opiates — that is who occupy and control addicts of the earth — Their point of entry is of course the drug itself — And they maintain this coordinate point through addiction" —

Question: "What determines the choice of coordinate points? Why does one controller operate through addiction in preference to other channels?" —

Answer: "He operates through addicts because he himself is an addict — A heavy metal addict from Uranus — What we call opium or junk is a very much diluted form of heavy metal addiction — Venusians usually operate through sexual practices — In short these controllers brought their vices and diseases from their planet of origin and infected the human hosts very much in the same way that the early colonizers infected so-called primitive populations" —

Question: "Inspector Lee, how can one be sure that someone purporting to be a nova police officer is not an impostor?" —

Answer: "It is not always easy, especially during this transitional period. There are imposters, 'shake men,' who haunt atomic installations and victimize atomic scientists in much the same way as spurious police officers extort money from sexual deviants in public lavatories — In one recent case a well-organized shake mob, purporting to represent the nova police, confiscated cyclotrons and other atomic equipment which they subsequently sold on the Uranian black market to support their heavy metal habits — They were arrested and sent away for the thousand year cure — Since then we have encountered a few sporadic cases — cranks, lunatics for the most part" —

Question: "Inspector Lee, do you think that the nova mob can be defeated?" —

Answer: "Yes — Their control machine has been disconnected by partisan activity —

"Now we can move in for some definitive arrests —

" 'Sammy the Butcher' dissolved his dummy cover —

His burning metal eyes stabbed at the officer from the molten core of a hot blue planet — The officer moved back dissolving all connections with the Blue Planet, connections formed by the parasite dummy which had entered his body at birth, carefully prepared molds and association locks closed on empty space — Sammy's eyes burned and sputtered incandescent blue and went out in a smell of metal — His last white-hot blast exploded in empty space — The officer picked up the microphone: 'Sammy the Butcher,' arrested — 'Paddy the Sting,' arrested — 'Hamburger Mary' has defected — 'Green Tony' has surrendered — move in for the definitive arrest of 'Mr Bradly Mr Martin' also known as 'Mr and Mrs D' also known as 'the Ugly Spirit' —

"'Sammy the Butcher' dissolved his ranks of self-righteous millions and stabbed at the officer dripping Marilyn Monroe Planet — Locks closed on empty space lettering 'My Fair Lady' — In three-dimensional terms 'The Ugly Spirit' and 'Mrs D' screamed through female blighted continent — So we turn over the Board Books and all the ugliness i had forgotten — criminal street — punitive legislation screaming for more association locks in electric chair and gas chamber — technical death over the land — white no-smell of death dripping nova — 'the Ugly Spirit' was flushed out of one host cover after the other — blanked out by our static and silence waves — Call the Old Doctor twice 'Mr and Mrs D' — He quiets you remember? — finished — no shelter — a handful of dust — Screaming, clawing for the nova switch 'the Ugly Spirit' was dragged from the planet — from all the pictures and words of ugliness that have been his place of residence since he moved in on the New World — The officer with silent inflexible authority closed one coordinate point after another — Only this to say: Would you rather talk to the partisans 'Mr and Mrs D' — Well? — No terms — This is definitive arrest — "Sammy the Butcher" has been taken — There are no guards capable protect you — Millions of voices in your dogs won't do you a bit of good — voices fading — crumpled cloth bodies — Your name fading across newspapers of the earth — Madison Avenue machine is disconnected — Errand boy closing their errand boys — Won't be much left — definitive arrest of the board as you listen, as the officer closes track — Self-righteous ugliness of their space program a joke — Written in symbols blighted America: $$$ — american scent of memory pictures — the idiot honky-tonks of Panhandle — humiliation outhouse and snarling ugliness of dying peoples — bourbon soaked legislators from 'marijuana is deadlier than cocaine' — board book symbol chains lynch mobs — the White Smoke pressure group relying on rectum suburbs and the no-smell of death — Control Avenue and Hollywood, look at the bread 'ine — The Ugly Spirit retreated back to the '20s in servants and police and the dogs of H. J. Anslinger — into one battered host after another — Blanked out board instructions —Silence — Silence — Silence — Call the old money equipment information files of memory — Finished — No shelter — A hand falls across newspapers of the earth for the nova switch — Won't do you a bit of good, collaborators with ugliness and degraded flesh — Traitors to all souls everywhere moved in on the New World — The Old Doctor cleaving a heavy silent authority closed one coordinate point after another — The board is near right now — Fading voice terms? — This is definitive arrest through dying air — There are no guards now capable guide humiliations — Poisonous cloud, millions of dogs won't do you a bit of good — parasites, crumpled cloth bodies — Your control books fading cross newspaper of the earth couldn't form nova — Operation completed — planet out of danger — Proceed with the indicated alterations' —

writing
machine

The Exhibition extended through many rooms and corridors — Booths spilled out into a composite garden formal sunken and terraced — Pools and canals reflected flower floats — (arrangements inextricably mixed with flower and garden pictures) —

In a room with metal walls magnetic mobiles under flickering blue light and smell of ozone — jointed metal youths danced in a shower of blue sparks, erections twisted together shivering metal orgasms — Sheets of magnetized calligraphs drew colored iron filings that fell in clouds of color from patterns pulsing to metal music, off on, on off — (The spectators clicked through a maze of turnstiles) — Great sheets of magnetized print held color and disintegrated in cold mineral silence as word dust falls from demagnetized patterns — Photomontage fragments backed with iron stuck to patterns and fell in swirls mixing with color dust to form new patterns, shimmering, falling, magnetized, demagnetized to the flicker of blue cylinders pulsing neon tubes and globes — In metal booths brain waves wrote the flickering message passed back and forth, over and through shifting grills — The magnetic pencil caught in calligraphs of Brion Gysin wrote back into the brain metal patterns of silence and space — orgone accumulators flickering blue over swimming tanks where naked youths bathed in blue — sound and image flakes falling like luminous grey snow — falling softly from demagnetized patterns into blue silence — Metal heads reversed eyes felt tingling blue spark erections — Metal orgasms flickering rainbow colors — came in wet scenic railways of dream — Electrodes from the brain wrote out boys on roller skates in a shower of ruined suburbs — Naked youths bathed in blue against the pinball machine danced and clicked — Old fashion plates falling like luminous snow falling softly dark-haired light-haired clicked deeper and deeper into the blue silence — The light travel machine is a revolving park turns around the traveler spilling metal music and nitrous fumes — Pinball acuteness twisted shivering in metal — Metal birds buzzed off in blue light — Jissom cartwheels in glass and mirrors reflected masturbating afternoons — (Naked youths bathed in blue distance now) — Flicker cylinders spill sandwich booths music and laughter across the water — Roller skates twisted in metal arcades — Pools and canals reflected grey suits carrying umbrellas — flickering over swimming boys as the magnetic silver light popped sound and image flakes — color writing a composite garden — layers peel off red yellow blue pools reflecting translucent tentative beings with flower hula hoops naked in blue twilight — metal youths shivering in stars and pool halls — In rooms flooded with sunlight panels of painting moved past each other on conveyor belts to music all the masters of the world past through each other in juxtapositions of light and color — Painting projected on screens mixed color and image — The Exhibition shaded into a vast amusement park with orchestras and rides and movie screens, stages and outdoor restaurants — All music and talk and sound recorded by a battery of tape recorders recording and playing back moving on conveyor belts and tracks and cable cars spilling the talk and metal music fountains and speech as the recorders moved from one exhibit to another — Vast mobile sculptures of music boxes and recorders wind chimes and movies of the exhibit reflected from ponds and canals and islands where restaurants enclosed in flicker cylinders spilled light and talk and music across the water — Plays on stage with permutating sections moved through each other Shakespeare, ancient Greek, ballet — Movies mix on screen half one half the other — plays in front of movie screen synchronized so that horses charge in and out of old Westerns — Characters walk in and out of the screen flickering different films on and off — Conversations recorded in movies taken during the exhibit appear on the screen until all the spectators are involved situations permutating and moving — (Since the recorders and movies of the exhibition are in constant operation it will be readily seen that any spectator 'appears on the screen sooner or later if not today then yesterday or tomorrow as the case may be in some connection — and repeat visitors of course —)

A writing machine that shifts one half one text and half the other through a page frame on conveyor belts — (The proportion of half one text half the other is important corresponding as it does to the two halves of the human organism) Shakespeare, Rimbaud, etc. permutating through page frames in constantly changing juxtaposition the machine spits out books and plays and poems — The spectators are invited to feed into the machine any pages of their own text in fifty-fifty juxtaposition with any author of their choice any pages of their choice and provided with the result in a few minutes.

You can say could give no information — dominion dwindling — We intersect on empty kingdom read to by a boy — Five times i made this dream — Consumed brandy neat, muttering in the last terrace of the garden — Light and shade departed have left no address — For i have known the body of a God bending his knees — Isn't time is there left? — The bitter foliage my friend to give you? — an odor of deluge and courage to let go — In the open air a boy waiting — Smiles overtake someone walking — The questions drift down slowly out of an old dream — mountain wind caught in the door — the odor of drowned suns trailing her linen sweat in the final ape of history — Like i'd ask alterations but blue sky on our ticket that exploded — any case a great leisure in the stern circumstances — Remember i was the ship and we drown — window rotting at the far end of creeks — The door couldn't reach flesh — naked dream beside you and the dreamer gone at dawn whisper — Put on a clean shirt and takes his way toward the sea —

"Written on the door pure information — Vast thing

police speak of a high condition, give you identity fading out — revolving lights is all — bread knife in the heart falling in the dark mutinous body without a shadow — Five times of dust we made it all — Relics give no shelter — dust trade — And those dogs knew nothing — Circumstances in the rawness of evening to give you? — smoke up the path — with such hair a colorless dreamer — brandy neat streaked with violence the door — solitude of morning washed to neon — Departed have left mixture of dawn and dream — leaning say good night under surges of silence, ebbing carbon dioxide" —

"Truly at this point many a one has failed — Mr Bradly Mr Martin is like pulp beside you — A man walks through dream shirt in another — Stopped suddenly to crown a God bending great sheets of magnetized U turn back to cool mineral silence — grey snow like bites of sunlight falling softly from noon — the naked good bye then silence — hints as we shifted masturbating afternoons through Ali's body — Magnetic silver flakes closed your account — nitrous screens crackling, genitals spilling scenic railways in sleep — Recorders of the city rotting — vast music in the throat of God — Movie screens went out from darkened restaurants — Dream and dreamer took their way flapping dead sections through each other — Juxtapositions of light made this dream — It has consumed image between the mirrors — and the naked good bye since the recorders' 1920 movie — (It will readily be seen nitrous flesh) — dust from demagnetized brain waves — The dreamer with dirty cheeks passes over streaked with violence — Pinball machines clicked wind chimes of subway dawns and turnstiles — roller skates, camp fire and red fuck lights reflected over swimming boys — old Westerns rotting at the far end of creeks — Blue notes drift through slate houses and nitrous fumes — jissom cartwheels in a sweetness of aging roots — Light layers peel off red yellow blue to crown tentative beings with flowers — spectral smell of naked ghost people — A maze of penny arcades and mirrors reflect masturbating afternoons — Color and image bloom out of an old dream in the odor of outdoor restaurants — Outside East St. Louis in the dominion of aging roots, ten-year-old keeping watch — Cracked pool hall and vaudeville voices made this dream — distant coffin between the mirrors of time that meanwhile i had forgotten — in a deserted cemetery the body of a God bending his knees — Yes you have his bitter skin" —

"Put it on — Without you i on pavement — Good bye in the open air — Someone walking trails my Summer dawn flesh" —

"Panama night pictures explode odor of naked rectums — sweat flipped from his face — milk in his crotch — Young faces melted dead nitrous streets — Naked brain splintered on empty flesh — bleeding dream and the dreamer is lying there — last round — the body without a shadow, without relics — breath of the trade winds on his face healed and half-healed, in the rawness of evening" —

"Like, man, good bye then — Silver film took it —"

The dreamer with dirty flesh strung together on scar impressions exploded in the kerosene lamp — open shirt flapping in the cool path — now calm his face — The street blew rain from solitude of morning, mixture of dawn and dream in doorways — surges of silence ebbing from the death trauma — Urine in the gutter weaves window people and sky picture through eyes of wine —

Evening blue over swimming tanks reflected ten-year-old keeping watch — in the kerosene lamp open shirt, erections — shivering knees twisted together — surges of silence ebbing from ruined suburbs — Naked youths came in wet sleep — windows people and sky like luminous flakes falling —

"Remember i was a battery of tape recorders at the door — Departed have left spectators involved — Good night under surges of silence since the recorders and movies in this point have failed — It will readily be seen beside you a man walks through screen — The exhibition reflected dominion dwindling — Photo flakes fell in swirls on our ticket — sound identity fading out — light travel — In this point many a one has failed — courage to go deeper and deeper into the blue — ebbing carbon dioxide — last terrace of the garden — Isn't time is there left? halves of the human organism to give you? —

substitute
flesh

The sex area of the amusement park can only be reached through channels — Anybody applying for entry must submit to naked photographic processing for ten days during which the applicant is photographed in all stages of erection, orgasm, defecation, urinating, eating — The pictures are cut down the divide line of the body and fitted to

other pictures of prospective partners — The photos vibrated and welded together in orgone accumulators* —
sex lines crossed and chartered so that memory tracks
merge and the area is already seen when the applicant
comes in — All sex acts that take place in the cubicles,
Turkish baths, scenic railways, ferris wheels and pools
where the subjects circulate in aqualungs are photographed and screens permutate partners divided down
the middle line until there is no way to distinguish film
from flesh and the flesh melts — For example two boys
fucking in front of a cubicle screen can see their pictures
developed after a few seconds and permutated with other
sex acts in other cubicles half one half the other shifting
back and forth speed-up slow-down line cutting the two
halves apart to neon — through the open window trailing
other pictures — Prospective ectoplasmic flakes welded

---

* Reference to the orgone accumulators of Doctor Wilhelm Reich —
Doctor Reich claims that the basic charge of life is this blue orgone-like
electrical charge — Orgones form a sphere around the earth and charge
the human machine — He discovered that orgones pass readily through
iron but are stopped and absorbed by organic matter — So he constructed
metal-lined cubicles with layers of organic material behind the metal —
Subjects sit in the cubicles lined with iron and accumulate orgones according to the law of increased returns on which life functions — The
orgones produce a prickling sensation frequently associated with erotic
stimulation and spontaneous orgasm — Reich insists that orgasm is an
electrical discharge — He has attached electrodes to the appropriate connections and charted the orgasm — In consequence of these experiments
he was of course expelled from various countries before he took refuge
in America and died in a federal penitentiary for suggesting the orgone
accumulator be used in treating cancer — It has occurred to this investigator that orgone energy can be concentrated to disperse the miasma
of idiotic prurience and anxiety that blocks any scientific investigation
of sexual phenomenon — Preliminary experiments indicate that certain
paintings — like Brion Gysin's — when projected on a subject produced
some of the effects observed in orgone accumulators —

together with a blue torch chartered the mattress twisted
and molded by absent memory tracks merged the masturbating afternoons — Reflected applicant enters and he
is already boy who owned that room stood naked with
erection permutations in his eyes — The sound and image
baths dusted his skin in sense withdrawal swirls where
the subject circulates through sensitized photos pulsing
telepathic communication — permutating the neck taped
on a silver line until the two being flesh melts body in
electric waves — rectums merging a few seconds after
blue movies and other sex acts with flicker ghosts shifting
back and forth orgasms of the world — tentative copulations of light down the dividing line — sound tracks
merged in a smell of KY and rectal mucus — A maze of
mirrors and screens reflected sex acts in slow motion to
a thousand sound tracks shifted and permutated — slow
waves of orgasm in a muttering sea of nitrous film flesh —
slow knees up to the chin now — prostates quivering in
pearly spasms — limestone flesh over silver pools — encrusted music releasing picture flares in moonlight — slow
smooth bodies to sound track of phallic statues — pulsing
human skin stuck to faces and pictures in scalpel flashes
— Adolescent ejaculated in a thousand cots — First spurts
he could feel the tip process together — Tentative being
struck drums of memory on his back vibrating focus flesh
— shifting erect penis and half-remembered skin instructions to accent of the attendant — thoughts and memories
of melting ice — the prostate quivering pearly spasms to
his penis in London hotel room — Adolescent lust ejaculated in stale underwear of penny arcades — The canals
reflected excitement slipping through legs — Cock flipped

out and up — Pearly spasms received and transmitted, nitrous flesh molded amber afternoons — Laughing suburb odors spatter out sound track — ejaculated in stale underwear filtered through encrusted odors of the world — Returning Mexican adolescent took my hand in room with a thousand cots — left muttering skin instructions to answer other thoughts and memories — Cock flipped out quivering in kerosene light — Old dead sound track shifting over you conceived in worn memory of first sex experience — Tingling implications try once more magnetic drums — Red nitrous odors spatter out sound track dummy to circumstance brown ankles — Ejaculated in stale underwear during execution, shirt flapping, pants slide — substitute excrement slipping through legs Almighty God with two coordinates immediately appropriate — We beg thy greased amber memory for the process — Pubic District Court vibrating focus flesh — half-remembered rectum on voluntary fertilizer tanks — youth grouped along the borders of melting ice — pearly spasms stirring skin instruction applicant — Dream flesh unexpectedly received and transmitted on smell of sewage denominationally molded to million dollar sale — at the earliest possible moment ejaculate in stale underwear almighty encrusted odor of three penises — Rapid calculations in room with a thousand cots warning combat troops — ejaculated with adequate military protection — First spurts touch intestine drums of memory — toothache punch cards muttering skin instructions written before explosion — Other thoughts and memories referred from quivering press statement — Adolescent lust broadcast over a thousand cots — What awaits you on substitute flesh? —

Bradly was met by a white-coated Cockney attendant he had known some years before in a London hotel room by Earl's Court —

"How are we? — Leave your gear here" —

He led Bradly to a room with metal walls that smelled of ozone and flash bulbs — Bradly stood naked under floodlights while the attendant took pictures — Full-length, close-ups, following the divide line down under his nose along his penis down to the rectum — The attendant made measurements chartering his body and wrote the numbers down in a note book —

"Full length now — That's right — Turn around — Bend over — Lie down — Knees up to the chin now" —

Bradly sat in a booth and electrodes were attached to his skull and penis and lips — He watched the wavering lines on a view screen jump and dance as the attendant touched him adjusting the electrodes — Small microphones were attached to the two sides of his body the sounds recorded on two tape recorders — He heard the beating of his heart, the gurgle of shifting secretions and food, the rattle of breath and scratches of throat gristle — crystal bubbles in the sinus chambers magnified from the recorders — The attendant ran the tape from one recorder onto the other to produce the sound of feedback between the two body halves — a rhythmic twang — soft hammer of heartbeats pounding along the divide line of his body — He ejaculated in a wet dream of scenic railways —

The attendant led him to a cubicle with cot, washstand, toilet and shower — He sat down on the cot with the attendant and the pictures just taken were flashed on a view screen that formed one wall of the cubicle —

"And now how are *we*?" —

Flashed a series of composites made by cutting Bradly's image down the middle and fitting to half-images of the attendant — Discrepancies smoothed out by vibrating focus scalpel of the projector until one body was picture in a series of positions —

"Full length now — That's right — Turn around — Bend over — Lie down — Knees up to the chin now" —

Lines of brain wave and electric discharge from erogenous zones appeared on screen shifted back and forth across each other in permutating grills welding two brains and bodies together with vibrating feedback — The screen shifted into a movie — Bradly was lying naked with the attendant on the cot — The divide line of his body burned with silver flash fire shifting in and out of the other body — rectal and pubic hairs slipping through composite flesh — penis and rectums merged on screen and bed as Bradly ejaculated — He woke up with other thoughts and memories in Cockney accent of that attendant standing there with a plate of food — saw himself eating on screen composite picture tasting food in the other mouth intestines moving and excrement squirming down to the divide line of another body—

Next day a Chinese attendant put Bradly through gymnastic positions on rings and hand-bars — the pictures repeated and cut in with composites of the attendant — tasting Chinese food the characters like neon in his throat — Other attendants: American, German, Spanish, Italian,

Arab, Negro — composites of all the attendants cut in together shifted and permutated through his body —

Now for the story of Bradly's clothes — painted human skin half-inflated — worn amber rectum valve at base of the spine — Attendant took pictures — Close-ups wrote the ticket to yellow and blue dawn trailing Pan pipes — Slow discrepancies smooth unknown bodies out the projector until one body of sex position to the sound track melted — Now turn around and bend over for the story of absent legs up to your chin — Mirror line of his body burned with second halves shifting erect penis and rectums — pulsing human skin stuck to faces half-remembered — vibrating focus scalpel flashes broken glaciers and skin instructions — He woke up with other thoughts i have touched in accent of the attendant — Pools and canals reflected excrement mixed with flowers — story of absent legs up the tarnished mirror — In a rusty privy youth bends over — faint drums of memory on his back — green boy of broken glaciers and skin instructions — encrusted music woke in jungle sounds of pools and canals cross the drenched lands — clouds of color under orange gas flares — worn amber memory of rectal swamps — Place exploded in muscles — First spurts he could feel the other body slipping all process together — Tentative being stuck to his penis half-remembered — Hyphenated line of his body shifting the applicant awoke — erect penis and rectum different — the story of penny arcades and dirty pictures — Unknown body slipped out of sex position to grow on us — Hairs rub the halves — Electric waves loosen you up a bit — other thoughts like luminous snow falling through London hotel room accent:

"How are we?" —

Timeless in flash bulbs here — Electrodes were attached in bath cubicles and locker rooms — Body burned with silver flash fire ejaculated in a few seconds — Flash bulbs along the penis popped sound and image flakes — The Other Half fades in mirror of beating heart — feedback sound of wind through the trees —

The sexual acrobats balance a chair on high wires and ejaculate from the tension — They masturbate from bicycles on the wire from tumbler pyramids and in the air of trapeze acts — (In the penny arcade he got a hard-on looking at the pictures and Hans laughed pointing to his fly — "Let's make the roller coaster" he said — We were the only riders and as soon as the car started we slipped off our shorts — We came together in the first dip as train roared up the other side throwing blood back into our drained genitals shirts flapping over the midway — boys swinging from rings and bars jissom falling through dusty air of gymnasiums — slide down into the pool of moldy jockstraps and chlorine ejaculating from the shock of water — ferris wheels falling silently through tumescent flesh) —

Bulletin from Rewrite: "The point of these exercises is to maintain a state of total alertness during sexual excitement — Try simple exercises first like jacking-off while balancing a chair — Driving full-speed on dangerous road — Flying plane — Performing precision operations at the same time like target shooting — So you can maintain alertness in the sex act and not be taken by the sex agents of the enemy who move to soften you up with sentimentality and sexual frustration to buy ersatz goo of their copy planet" —

The two boys got in the cub naked and took off climbing to an altitude of two thousand feet with dual controls — Hans put the plane into a spin while the other boy jacked him off — slipping, looping, ejaculated from the shift of blood came in with a hard-on for a spot landing — shooting coins flipped into the air cock pulsing in the afternoon sun —

Bradly moved into a maze of orgone accumulators — circular rooms lined with magnetic iron — He entered the maze with three other boys — In the first chamber they found iron frames on which they stretched their bodies in different positions ˵of exposure — A vibrating silence hummed through the magnetized air — Tingling blue light touched his rectum and genitals playing along the divide line left a taste of metal in the mouth — Smaller accumulators with hose attachments turned directly on erogenous zones the message of orgasm received and transmitted — He passed now to other rooms with magnetized sex symbols on revolving walls — The three other boys were not there now — They had been replaced by precise copies in a substance like flexible amber molded from their bodies, the two halves welded together — Odors spattered out as electric vibrators sidled the dummies toward him — smell of rectal mucus, sweat, carbolic soap, jissom, and stale underwear over clean young flesh — From transistor radios in the throat drifted all the sex words of his wet dreams and masturbating afternoons — The penis canal was a jointed iron tube covered by sponge rubber — Pubic hairs of fine wire crackled with blue sparks — The dummy cocks rose in response to magnetic attraction of the wall symbols — "Bend over" Bradly stretched himself over an iron frame — The dummy that was precisely *me* penetrated him with a slow magnetic movement — Tingling blue fire shot through his genitals transfixed by the magnetic revolving wall symbols — The vibrator switched on as the others watched — idiot lust drinking his jissom from screen eyes — Sucking cones of color that dissolved his penis in orgasms of light —

"Better than 'the real thing?' — There is no real thing — Maya — Maya — It's all show business" —

Picture flesh — felt the penny arcade in his crotch — fly full of dust, pulled up his pants — back into drained genitals — Intersection of these exercises spattered light on total alertness during sexual flight — naked for physical riders as stomach muscles exploded in altered pressure — "Whee" the sex act soften you up to buy death in orgasm of copy planet — Other side throwing the orgone accumulators — take over all sexual apparatus — smell of moldy jockstraps and chlorine ejaculating —

Bulletin from Rewrite: "Sex is electric output of the organism in message received and transmitted — Sex words evoke a dangerous that is to say *other* half of the body — Precise attraction — So what is ejaculation? Shooting at target — The orgasm is a flash bulb that takes your picture — Charge of course is electrical hose attachments they turned on — Rusty image of a separate being — feed-back noise of accumulators — You see the caustic layers of organic material? That is what they need from earth: Three other boys to make more marble flesh, ass and genitals vibrated by the iridescent attendant — Orgasm death is to other half of the body — So what is ejac-ulation? substitute patterns twisting through electrical pubic hairs, feed-back throat hum, recorder jack-off — Hose attachment substitutes all cocks — They turned off nervous system to the metal ray — switch on off body sound magnetic patterns — Where 'the passengers' came together recorders jack-off in flash coordinates — back into your drained genitals all junk and cool circuits — Virus punch cards waiting before organism — 8276 runs out in iridescent road naked with a hard-on shooting torture films — Maintain your alertness in eyes glinting with slow fish lust — sex agents of the enemy who color sex words with ersatz goo — pass along the orgone in throat gristle alternating body — take a simple tape from one hum between the hose attachments — Orgones through iron repetition setting off word tape response in the other nervous system—image of a separate being touched lungs penis and electric body hairs — now passes along orgone in throat gristle alternating sex words to color: 'Bradly' entered the controlled prisoner body — tingling blue light in a simple tape from one drifting hum for the act between hose attachments — layers of organic material rubbing off the encrusted odors of three other boys and so a 'conversation' that has ass and genitals spelt out in his mouth — ejaculation output of control system received and transmitted — Sex words evoke the other open shirt flapping viscera — torture films electric eyes glinting with insect lust — alternating amber beads and little tunes taken centuries to accrete — hum and taste of metal in the beads — Stroking music from hose attach-ments they turn virus punch cards to magnetic patterns —

past time energy units — That is to say a *dead land* — 8276 whispered through iron from pale word dust stirring tape — marble parasite image of a separate being — dream flesh held together by sex words" —

The Sex Musicians drift through streets of music trailing melodious propositions — In bath cubicles of a rotting pier over tide flats a boy played the jade flute while Bradly screwed him following the notes out of his body into birdcalls lapping water and distant music on the trade winds — In a cool blue room sucked off a clarinet player to a climax of wind chimes, subway dawns, and clicking turnstiles — Under red fuck lights bent over a black hotel chair beating a drum as a Mexican boy with street dust in his hair fucked him to the drumbeats — these sounds recorded and carried through streets of music — The Sex Musicians drift in and out of combos as colored light pulses to their instruments — on a rotting pier: "Here goes" — Bradly bent over a chair and spread ass cheeks — Smoke finger fucked him to drumbeats — as colored light pulsed through old photos turning sex words and singing dust — ghost rectums drum and pipe to silence from satellite rings — The units turn faster and faster through streets of music trailing word dust over the tide flats — Faster played the flute — Here goes word dust planet — his body into birdcalls and distant music on the wind — "I wanta screw you" in a cool room with rose wallpaper — faces naked of word dust in a shower of ruined suburbs — rings of Saturn in the morning sky as a Mexican boy stirred slow rectum gate — "Want screw you — Over" — "Here goes" — Spin the walls and orbit sex words back to color — Played the flute in flash bulb of orgasm — tarnished mirror of subway dawns in the bath cubicle — "Bend over" — sex words back to slow movement of rivers — young faces lapping water — wind chimes from Attic frieze — drumbeats of ghost people — "You is coming?" into birdcalls and jungle sounds — In red light felt his pants slide — Cock flipped out and up — Beat a drum on knees like *como perros* — "Slow, deep, Johnny" — The notes twisting Johnny's thighs — candle shadow bent over a chair — Fucked to music from the casino — flicker faces and bodies fade-out in old photos — toilet smell of subway dawns — Greek vases give out slow crystal music of phallic statues and limestone centuries — Played the flute with fingers light and cold over my naked body — City sounds drift through a blue room under the slate roof — penny arcades on the rotting pier — "Here goes" — flesh sparks to drumbeats — Played the flute faster and faster — limestone flesh stirring in old movies — Hairs rub the rose wallpaper — "You wanta screw me?" trailing flash bulb of orgasm in other flesh — "You is coming?" — pale smell of dawn rectums over a chair — Questions pulse to their instruments — rings of Saturn in the morning sky — Fucked to ebbing carbon dioxide — "Mr Bradly Mr Martin" is smell of subway dawns — Played the flute with fingers light and cold in the door — City sounds drift through the final ape of history —

"Remember i was the movies, the door flash bulb of orgasm — sex words in the cold Spring air — pale smell of dawn shirt — distant proposition in bath cubicles, there the boy played a flute, ten-year-old keeping watch — cracked out of his body into birdcalls and vaudeville voices — distant music to crown a God with street dust

— in the gutter urine sounds — naked brain stranded in the tide flats — Fade-out overtakes a rotting pier — Young faces turn faster and faster through dead nitrous streets — open shirt in the bath cubicle — The street blew rain — You is coming in the death trauma?" —

Distant coffin pulses to their instruments — odor of naked rectums on the rotting pier — "Here goes" in his crotch — Here goes word dust planet — faces naked of old dream — Rings of Saturn in the morning sky melted sex words back to color — Tarnished mirror of subway dawns lying there — Last round over — sex words back to the trade winds — rose wallpaper bleeding dream — Clicking turnstiles left no address — For i have known street dust in his hair — "Isn't time is there left to give you" — A boy waits on the rotting pier — Departed have left distant music from the casino — over the water "good night" in old photo — sleep breath under the slate roof — solitude of morning stirring old limestone flesh — Leaning say: "You is coming? — ebbing carbon dioxide — Man, like good bye then — Remember i was movies — Played the flute in last terrace of the garden — City sounds drift through a blue room — Left no address — For i have known arcades on the rotting pier — Isn't time is there left? — Played the flute faster and faster to you — Sex words drifted slowly out into the cold Spring air — pale smell of dawn in the door — Played the flute with fingers fading" —

hands of light in the morning sky — rotting mummy moved out at dawn — The doctor on stage — end of the line —

"All right, doctor, before stranded in the tide flats indications enough — i told you i would heal scars — i am the big fix talking of orbit on scar impressions — Suddenly shut off in the gutter urine sounds, all the Garden of Delights — God of Panic piping blue notes — invisible intervention — last round over — last parasite muttering there: 'Man, like good bye then' " —

Memory pictures and singing dust went up in slow motion — Scandinavia outhouse skin forgotten — rings of Saturn in the morning sky — errand boy of subway dawns remitted back to the trade winds — slow silence ebbing from centuries — rose wallpaper bleeding youth body without a shadow — smell of dawn flesh in a privy — precise identity fading out — And these boys circumstance the orgasm leaving — beat a drum twisting Johnny's healed scars — over the pass without doing pictures — all toilet smell at this point — tarnished mirror through dying peoples — words back to the trade winds — errand boy remitted — leaning say "Good bye — fading my name — silence in tarnished offices — last rotting pier — Isn't time — the Doctor on stage — end of the line — Played the flute in empty room, fingers fading — Doctor on stage — Played the flute in last errand boy — Closing — Left no address" —

"All right, doctor, before silence indications enough — i told you i would come — Silence healed scars" —

Bradly stood naked with ten subjects in a room lined with metal mirrors — They helped each other into loose fitting cellophane envelopes — A trap door opened in the floor of the cubicle — and the subjects lowered themselves into the sense withdrawal tank and floated a few feet apart in darkness with no sound but* feedback from the two halves of ten bodies permutated to heartbeat body music vibrating through the tank — Body outlines extend and break here — The stretching membrane of skin dissolves — Sudden taste of blood in his throat as gristle vaporizes and the words wash away and the halves of his body separated like a mold — Fish sperm drifted through the tank in silent explosions — Skeletons floated and crab parasites of the nervous system and the grey cerebral dwarf made their last attempt to hold prisoners in spine and brain coordinates — screaming "You can't — You can't — You can't" — Screaming without a throat without speech centers as the brain split down the middle and the feed-back sound shut off in a blast of silence.

His body extend and break here — He watched the wavering stretching membrane of skin jump and dance to rhythmic feed-back noise from the electrodes — Magnified sperm drifted through water tape in silent explosions — flash fire shifting hairs through composite outline — a sudden taste of blood on screen as Bradly vaporized the words — Other thoughts and memories

---

* The most successful method of sense withdrawal is the immersion tank where the subject floats in water at blood temperature, sound and light withdrawn — Loss of body outline, awareness and location of the limbs occurs quickly, giving rise to panic in many American subjects — Subjects frequently report feeling that another body is floating half-in and half-out of the body in the first part — Experiments in sense withdrawal using the immersion tanks have been performed by Doctor Lily in Florida — There is another experimental station in Oklahoma — So after fifteen minutes in the tank these Marines scream they are losing outlines and have to be removed — I say put two marines in the tank and see who comes out — Science — Pure science — So put a marine and his girl friend in the tank and see who or what emerges —

separated like a mold — half-remembered dissolving skin instructions — Cellophane membrane over absent legs outline his body with second halves — Encrusted music separated like a mold — First spurts he could feel outline together — hyphenated line of amoebic process — Hairs rub the skin membrane jump "I wanta screw you" from the electrodes —

"Here goes Johnny — His body extend and break here — One track out" — Clear erection stretching membrane of skin — Film track feed-back noise of rectal mucus and carbolic soap — Pale heartbeats through his body — all process in the throat — Sick dawn smell of sperm drifting through water on all cocks in silent explosion — genital night of black fruit that grows dream flesh — Heartbeats wrote the numbers through his body: blood in throat gristle "That's right — His body extend and break here — Knees up to the chin now" —

Bulletin from the Rewrite Department: "Now look, you jokers — We are not here to rewrite G.O.D. (Garden Of Delights) you got it? Watch those fuckers — Still on the old evacuation plan" —

throat gristle sex words on two halves of the body — vibrating the spinal column — shared meals contract of rectum flight — metal hairs falling like dry leaves — crystal body music vibrating the two recorders — screaming neon in the throat — worn amber body music — They fade out in old photos here —magnified present time tape in silent explosions — past time units whirl evening faces into drifting smoke and dead land of black lagoons — a slow whisper in his brain — The units turn faster and faster — Full length now —Washed green light from penis and lips — His body attendant break here — Here goes Word Dust Planet and crab parasites —

("Now for me — The story of two halves — other parasite possessing every possible out for this painting — first it's Symbiosis Door Con — There are no good relationships — There are no good words — I wrote silences — a storm leaving his brain centers — evening faces into the ponds — I wept in a land of black lagoons and skies — crumbling stone villas — green-black fruit that grows in jars — lonely lemur calls in ruined courtyards — ghost hands at paneless windows — ancient beauty in stone shapes") —

Hospital smells and the wooden numbness of anesthesia — He saw his body on an operating table split down the middle — A doctor with forceps was extracting crab parasites from his brain and spine — and squeezing green fish parasites from the separated flesh —

"My God what a mess — The difficulty is with two halves — other parasites will invade sooner or later — First it's symbiosis, then parasitism — The old symbiosis con — Sew him up nurse" —

the
black fruit

Lykin lay gasping in the embrace of the fishboy who was gently tugging at the space suit, running delicious cold fingers down his spine — Finally it found a hold and ripped the tough material in one violent tear right up the back — Lykin, who had so far not been exposed to the atmosphere of the planet, found himself choking as though ice claws were tearing his insides apart — A great smothering blackness descended on him and he fell back in the boy's arms, unconscious —

He was drifting through space, wafted by currents of glowing gases — Myriads of floating forms passed in front of him some familiar and others alien — For a moment he was back in the brown canals of Mars in the grip of a giant clam, which takes a week to satisfy its consuming sex habit and spits out its unfortunate victim covered with its discharge like a gelatinous pearl on the dry red sands —

Thousands of voices muttered out of the darkness, twittering creatures pulling and tugging at him and dancing on their way leaping from soaring black heights into deep blue chasms trailing the neon ghost writing of Saturn through vast wells of empty space — From an enormous distance he heard the golden hunting horns of the Aeons and he was free of a body traveling in the echoing shell of sound as herds of mystic animals galloped through dripping primeval forests, pursued by the silver hunters in chariots of bone and vine —

Lonely lemur calls whispered in the walls of silent obsidian temples in a land of black lagoons, the ancient rotting kingdom of Jupiter — smelling the black berry smoke drifting through huge spiderwebs in ruined courtyards under eternal moonlight — ghost hands at the paneless windows weaving memories of blood and war in stone shapes — A host of dead warriors stand at petrified statues in vast charred black plains — Silent ebony eyes turned toward a horizon of always, waiting with a patience born of a million years, for the dawn that never rises — Thousands of voices muttered the beating of his heart — gurgling sounds from soaring lungs trailing the neon ghost writing — Lykin lay gasping in the embrace can only be reached through channels running to naked photographic process — molded by absent memory, by vibrating focus scalpel of the fishboy gently in a series of positions running delicious cold fingers "Stand here — Turn around — Bend" — Ripped the tough material in brain waves — Lykin who had not so far been on screen of the planet found himself choking, the two brains tearing his insides apart — Smothering from the four halves and he fell back in the boy's arms naked on the space bed wafted by currents glowing in and out shifting forms passed in front of him — Body burned with silver flash for a moment he was back in the brown rectal hairs of a giant clam — halves shifting and permutating out of the darkness — He drifted off into deep blue chasms and memories of Saturn — vast faces and pieces of distance — He heard the golden medium and was free of his body — Touched hunting horns of the Aeons silver hunters in chariots with flowers — picture temples in a land of black food — ghost hands twisted together in stone shapes —

Found himself choking as unknown bodies tear his insides apart — Wafted by currents of glowing halves shifting mist in electric waves — gelatinous rectal swamps fermenting darkness —

He drew the black berry smoke deep into his lungs and symbol language of an ancient rotting kingdom bloomed in his brain like Chinese flowers — myriads of floating sex symbols and the bronze flesh familiar — Now thousands

of voices muttered and pulsed through him pulling tearing — His body trailed the neon ghost writing as the two
halves separated and sex words exploded to empty space
— Lonely lemur calls whispered his knees up to the chin
— smelling black movement of the other in ruined courtyards — slow color orgasm under ghost hands reflected
on silent obsidian walls — The ancient rotting kingdom
softened and glowed with black berry smoke drifting
through pubic hairs under eternal moonlight to dust and
shredded memories — pale word dust stirring spider webs
from penis and lips — weaving memories of blood in his
throat — rectum naked to color focus of the fish language
running delicious cold fingers rubbing off encrusted odors
in slow turns of amber — glowing torture films in a land
of black food — Ghost apes tear his insides apart — He
was in a ruined garden under two moons — one red the
other a pale clear green — He could see pulsing black
fruit growing in crystal jars — In front of him stood a
young man molded in polished black bronze with streaks
of green patina on the high cheekbones — From the lips,
half-open in a dreamy cruel smile, drifted a faint smell of
decay as if he were rotting inside the bronze mold —
With a slow gesture he led Bradly along a path of cracked
flagstones — Bradly saw that he had webbed feet leaving
prints of silver slime that glittered in the moonlight —
They came to a summerhouse of circular shape over-
grown with vines from which dangled the black fruit in
crystal jars — The summerhouse was lined with a glistening black substance traced with phosphorescent writing in blue metal that filled the room with a pulsing blue
twilight — The guide focused projector pupils talking in

color blasts to some other being Bradly could feel stirring response in the liquid medium of his body — Color flashed through his body in chirps and giggles shifting to slow visceral pulses — Still talking to the other inside, the bronze boy put slow cold hands on Bradly's shoulders — As the metal hands drew him forward his clothes shredded to dust — He caught a faint whiff of decay like tropical fruit on the wind — His body melted from within — The bronze mold sank into his flesh a black seal — The other moved back seeking some precise coordinate point with the blue wall symbols — The room hummed and vibrated — Pubic hairs of black wire crackled in blue sparks and a quivering blue line divided his body — Bradly felt his own body split down the middle like a cracked egg the two halves rubbing against each other, held together by some sticky gelatinous substance that leaked out the crack and dripped into the obsidian platform where he stood — From the open bronze mold emerged a transparent green shape crisscrossed with pulsing red veins, liquid screen eyes swept by color flashes — a smell of sewage and decay breathing from years of torture films, orgasm death in his black eyes glinting with slow fish lust of the swamp mud — Long tendril hands penetrated Bradly's broken body caressing the other being inside through the soft intestines into the pearly genitals rubbing centers of orgasm along his spine up to the neck — Exquisite toothache pain shot through his nerves and his body split down the middle — Sex words exploded to a poisonous color vapor that cut off his breath — The floor dropped away beneath his feet and he fell into black water with the green creature twisted deep into his flesh, vine tendrils twisted round the throat — Green flares exploded his brain — He ejaculated in twisting fish spasms knees up to the chin — a taste of blood as fish syllables tore gills in his throat — He was breathing now in a silent medium — slow color orgasms deep in the iridescent lagoon — long tendril pubic hairs caressing other memory, vibrated dead genitals — weaving orgasm deep in his testicles — twisting in slow marble ghost hands — gathering stone shape —

He moved through shadow alleys and canals of the lagoon city — fish smells and dead eyes in doorways — sound of fear — dark street life of a place forgotten — slow memory bubbles bursting in his brain — broken picture warnings — grey foetal lampreys along the canal walls, crab police with magnetic claws, dungeons where the prisoners are broken to insect forms under cruel idiot fingers of the Green Guards, slim elegant men with smooth brown flesh the color of an eel's side hand ending in a crystal bulb and a dripping stinger: the Orgasm Sting that twists a victim to quivering pulp eaten by cruising Mugwumps with beaks of black bone and purple penis flesh — The Mugwumps milked for the orgasm meal by vampire women embalmed in predigested sperm, faces of smooth green alabaster giving off a smell of phosphorus as they sip spinal fluid through straws — He felt now the weakness of death in his fading larval flesh — He needed "The Slow Boat To China" — He found his way to "The Flower Market" where the nobles cruise languidly in gondolas of paper-thin black wood watching slow color bubbles of the fishboys climb to the surface and burst in flares of iridescent propositions — An answer vibrated down through the water: "Two Black Fruit" — Thin and no conditions to bargain he bubbled back: "It's a deal" surfaced and slid into a gondola where a young man lay naked on a bed of flowers — His legs were amputated at the hip and the stumps glowed with slow metal fires — The fishboy lay down beside the young man — His translucent green penis rose pulsing in the moonlight — Negro boys the color of glistening black tar beat little drums from a dais in the center of the lagoon — Lonely lemur calls drifted from islands of swamp cypress — Slow rocket burst over the water — They rolled on the flower bed crushing out clouds of odor — color fingers through his larval flesh feeling along his fish spine — Spasms shook his body and green erogenous slime poured from glands under his gills covering the two bodies with a viscous bubble — softening flesh and bones to jelly — He sank into the client — Spines rubbed and merged in little shocks of electric pleasure — He was sucked into other testicles — A soft pearly grotto closed round him pulsing tighter and tighter — He melted to sperm fingers caressing the penis inside — Quivering contractions as he squirmed through pink tumescent flesh to a crescendo of drumbeats shot out in a green flare falling into slow convolutions of underwater sleep —

Shifting dominion of the other inside — bronze mold blooms slowly from old dream odors trailing sweat of genitals before daybreak — slow orgasm in green roses — What you have loved remains stirring response in the fading body — naked pubic hairs caressing dream and the dreamer weaving orgasm in his ghost hands —

Coffin put slow cold hands on Bradly — body split

down the middle like sunlight and shadow — (Have you lost your dog?) — leaked out the crack of dead nitrous flesh — Sex words exploded to a poisonous sky — raw testicles twisting in slow marble — the evening you hear shredded to dust — last terrace of the garden in rotting fruit — dawn whisper knees up to the chin — Who is speaking? — Memory vibrated dead genitals without names — crackling paper shredded to dust —

"For i have known fires — Isn't time is there left, cool finger running on our ticket that exploded, larval circumstances at far end of the creek? And these dogs knew nothing shifting the dominion of circumstances — What bronze mold blooms in aging roots? — response in the fading body beside you?" —

Could give no response in words — his body melted from within — crumpled cloth flapping wind —

Could have indications enough man lay on a bed of flowers — The stumps glowed with slow metal good bye on vacant lots — smell of healed and half-healed genitals — penis pulsing in the dog rotation — the bronze sweetness of khaki pants — feeling cool fingers on his naked dollars — larval erogenous face spurting out through orgasm —

"Talk, Face" —

"I'm just a vagabond along his spine and feeling well as you, darling — a biologic from viscous bubble with the St. Louis suburb" — I had a dog rubbed and merged to drumbeats open shirt flapping — shadow eggs through the other penis slowly reformed in delicious naked boy — (See that the client is satisfied this time?) —

'Twas good bye on the line — since you went slowly
out of old dream odors into space —

Bradly's canoe of paper-thin black wood grounded on
an island of swamp cypresses — He strapped on his
camera gun and walked along ancient paths and stone
bridges over canals where the fish people swirled sending
up color bubbles of orgasm that broke on the iridescent
surfaces — He caught the twittering chirping sound of
the tree-frog people like wind chimes in the trees and one
of them leaped down from an overhanging branch and
attached itself to his chest with sucker paws — It was
about two feet in length of a translucent green color —
The obsidian eyes were all pupil and mirrored a pulsing
blood suction to rhythms of a heart clearly visible in the
transparent flesh — A network of veins filtered through
the green substance like red neon tubes suffusing the frog
boy with a phosphorescent pink light — The mouth above
a small pointed chin was of glistening black gristle that
dripped a pale yellow saliva — Others leaped down from
the dark cypress chirping and giggling — Sucker fingers
unstrapped his gun and pulled down his shorts — Naked
he lay down in warm swamp mud that gave slowly under
him stirring a black smell of decay — He felt the soft
mouth close over his penis and hang there pulsing, sucking his body to a vacuum — Earth and water stones and
trees poured into him and spurted out broken pictures —
The creature dropped off and rolled itself into a foetal ball
of sleep — Bradly picked up another and held it in his
hands — The creature vibrated like a radio — Little
shocks ran up Bradly's arms — The frog boy kicked in
spasms ejaculating spurts of black liquid that gave off a

musty smell of damp roots, jasmine and sewage — Now he hung limp in sleep eyes veiled by green lids like a black pond covered with delicate algae — And Bradly fell slowly into the deep uterine sleep, frog boys curled between his legs and under his arms and on his chest streaked with iridescent slime from their sucker paws —

He woke to drifting golden notes of distant hunting horns — He sat up — The frog people were gone — The horns were louder and clearer now — Into the clearing where he sat burst a pack of dogs with human skin and faces — The animals were the size and shape of small greyhounds — They surrounded him snarling and yapping — A young man appeared standing in a weightless medium so that his feet made no impression in the swamp mud — Naked except for a quiver of silver arrows and a bow, he radiated a calm disdainful authority — He lifted a slow hand and the dogs were silent — He looked at Bradly with something too neutral to be called contempt and spoke in English: "I see that the blockade is broken and we expect such visitors — Street boys fed on scraps and garbage" —

The dogs were smiling and whimpering now rubbing against Bradly, squirming and ejaculating under his fingers — The young man looked at the dogs and he looked at Bradly — He smiled a slow smile old as the rotting kingdom — "Well, Mr Bradly, we shall see" — He picked up Bradly's camera gun — Looked at it from a vast distance and dropped it into the mud — Several bearded naked huntsmen had entered the clearing carrying long golden horns —

"Come, Mr Bradly — There is much for you to learn

and quickly — Otherwise you must assume some form acceptable to the Old Controller — Your present form is quite intolerable, of course — No, you won't need your clothes" —

They came to a palace of crumbling stone covered by trailing vines from which dangled the glistening black fruit in jars — a ruined garden decorated with phallic statues — The Prince stopped before two marble youths kneeling in the act of sodomy their faces turned up to the eternal moonlight remote and dreamy with slow pleasure of limestone centuries — As Bradly watched they shifted in a slow movement and a pearl stood out on the boy's erect penis, glittered in the moonlight — The bronze statue of a masturbating boy yielded a drop of phosphorescent black ichor — "That is where the Black Fruit comes from — Then it is grafted into the vines and it must ripen in the jars until it is ready" — There were other statues of silver and gold and porcelain all yielding the slow fruit of time — They were walking now along ruined porticoes where youths of translucent amber caressed each other stroking out encrusted odors and whiffs of music —

all members
are worst
a century

"Ward Island is afflicted by a disease so terrible that the entire ceremonial life of the natives revolves around fear of the disease and precautions to avoid it — The onset is sudden — The victim is seen abusing himself publicly while addressing some unseen presence with endearing terms — He becomes dirty and emaciated — In the final stages he is literally eaten alive by his invisible partner and subsides into the state of an insect larva paralyzed, slobbering and covered by a caustic green slime that seeps from the rectum — In this condition they are carried out into the mud flats by the superstitious natives and left to the mercy of land crabs — (Note: This practice has been forbidden by the resident governor) — The island is almost level with the water and surrounded by shallow lagoons so that boats must anchor about two miles off shore" —

So writes an early traveler — It was evening when the boat anchored and i could see nothing of the island — i had my equipment for the expedition packed and my boy Jimmy helped me to load it into a gondola of thin black wood — The boatman was a young man with the lithe frame of a Malay and bright red lips — He kept his eyes cast down with the closed beaten expression of dying peoples — He propelled us through iridescent oily water that gave off a rank odor under his strokes — We tied up at a rotting pier that extended out into the shallow water — Sting rays and crabs stirred clouds of black mud — We were met at the pier by a middle-aged Dutchman who was proprietor of the only hotel — He led the way along a wooden catwalk to the hotel which was a three story structure of split bamboo on high stilts over the swampy ground — Darkness was falling and after unpacking we descended to the veranda and had a whisky with the proprietor — i asked him about the disease — "It is here

in the head — So they are scaring themselves to the death
— i am now twenty years here — In other times we used
to export much fruit that grow here — So a special fruit
black with such a taste — Then these stupid stories come
out and the island is now quarantine" —

When i told him of my plan to make an expedition to
the interior of the island he said it would be impossible
to obtain any native guides or bearers since the disease
is supposed to have its origin in the swamps and jungles
of the interior —

July 7, 1862 — Saw something of the island and the
natives — Surrounding the hotel is a village crisscrossed
with catwalks over the mud flats — The entire island
seems to consist of swamp delta — The natives are silent
and sad conveying the impression of faded photos — As
the proprietor predicted we were unable to enlist any
native guides or boatmen — With his help we have pur-
chased one of the flat gondolas — with an outrigger attachment and mats of split bamboo we can pitch our tent
over the boat — We will start for the interior tomorrow —

July 8, 1862 — We got an early start poling and pad-
dling our canoe up the river — There seems to be little
wild life about — nothing but swamp with here and there
islands of swampy ground and cypress — At twilight we
tied up to a cypress stump and put out our night lines —
After a meal of tinned food we spread the mat of split
bamboo and lay down under mosquito netting — The
night pressed against our naked bodies like a damp mold
spread to jungle sounds and lapping water — Am writing
this at dawn —

July 9, 1962 — Disease of the image track — The onset

is sudden voices screaming a steady stream — I had forgotten unseen force of memory pictures — Muttering slobbering outhouse skin seeps from his rectum — island of dying people surrounded by shallow lagoons — The boatman smiles — Wired red lips entered the '20s in drag from the Ward Island natives — slow motion through iridescent oily water — Absent tenants stood naked — Ghost disease spattered on victim — Muttering to himself interrogates substance of the other invisible presence — He becomes dirty with the speed of "Want it" — Tentative being eaten alive by empty flesh of insect larvae — Human form been covered by caustic green slime — Faces sucked into other land that is almost level with the water — Passengers are picked up by flicker — It was early morning when mummy fingers goosed his ass — round gate from burning sex skin — wind voices beside the man with lithe frame of a Malay — Sullen female impersonators listen — the faces all forgotten — Orgasm of memory strokes gave off a rank smell under his law — Prisoners in the terminal case carried to crabs — mummy flesh over middle-aged deflated skin — death's own boy — talk to switchblade of bamboo — Business dissolved in smoke and errand boy of such a taste — "All right, Doctor, quarantined" he gestures at indications enough "i told you i would come naked on our beds — Healed scars cry from Jimmy saying he had to pass without doing pictures — i found enemy all right — Suddenly shut off excitement" —

July 9, 1862 — We pulled in our night lines and found a large fish with a smooth yellow skin — The meat was soft and phosphorescent and had a metallic taste — In the late afternoon we grounded the boat on a sand bar and got out to bathe in a shallow pool that came up to our ankles — As Jimmy was rubbing soap on my back we noticed an orchid covered by brilliant green and red flowers hanging over the water — As we touched the plant long tendrils covered by erectile hairs stung our necks and shoulders — A burning itch ran over my body exploding in rectum and genitals like liquid fire — With an animal cry Jimmy forced his soapy penis into my rectum — We fell rolling and i ejaculated into the soft swamp mud — We lay there panting — Simultaneously we were both attacked by a scalding diarrhea — The burning itch swelled our tongues and lips — Clawing screaming we twisted in water brown with excrement, ejaculating again and again — bone wrenching spasm that popped silver light in our eyes —

July 11 ? 12 ? 13 ? 1862 — Sinking deeper and deeper into sexual deliriums — obsessed by fantasies of hanging and death in orgasm — Once in India i saw a young man hanged — His loin cloth slipped off in the drop and he hung there naked twisting in bone wrenching spasms, ejaculated again and again his feet rustling weeds under the gallows —

We are both emaciated now — The entire pool is brown with our excrement — Is Jimmy really there? — He is turning into a phantom woman with red hair and green flesh — i woke in the moonlight to find — her entwined around my body — She opened her mouth and tendrils covered by stinging red hairs squirmed out penetrating my mouth and throat, feeling into my rectum and penis, twisting around the spine touching electric centers of orgasm in the neck that popped silver light in my eyes —

The creature was pointing now to the tie-up rope that trailed from our boat — In a flash i realized that if i followed her obvious suggestion i would be eaten body and soul by the orchid people — i summoned the strength to resist — Tomorrow i will make an attempt to leave the orchid pool —

July 11, 12, 13, 1962 — Present time leads to an understanding of knowing and open food in the language of life — the entire dia through noose in four letter words — It will be seen that "havingness" muttering in the night — Went back other identities — Remember my medium of false identities? — All that links the murders is Game Hate Box — Opponents are future time 1962 — The donar was released folk singer Logos — Uncontrolled flash bulbs popped — It is a grand feeling — Language of virus (which *is* these experiments) really necessary? Message of life written "We have come to eat"? ? —

i have said the basic time to go — Everyone here: knowing officers at the delicate lilt — all dia through noose with just the right shade of absolute need — condition empty but process known as "overwhelming" — Flak holes told him that "havingness" unknown and hostile land — The Cycle of Action: the Cycle of Venus — sickness of hunger — flesh naked for the delicate lilt — clear fingers in stale New Zealand — Assailant of sleep in the naked Panama night was such a deal — Shadow passing and transparent lodging is not done abruptly — *Unknown and hostile land — we* are all parasites of the area — i have said basic time to go — Wind of morning disintegrates present time —

July 14, 1862 — i woke up in the silent dripping dawn

— i was lying beside the boat and as i watched little grey
men played on the deck hoisting invisible sails — They
formed a chorus line and danced away into the dawn
mist pointing as they faded out to a dangling vine — i got
up and stripped leaves and bark from the vine and brewed
a tea — i drank the tea from a tin cup — Almost immediately i vomited so violently that my body seemed to crack
open — i leaned against the boat panting and gasping —
Slowly my whole being fused to incandescent resistance
— A young male face of dazzling beauty moved in and i
was free of my body — The orchid girl floated over the
pool toward me and i rushed her stuttering back sex words
that tore her tentative substance like bullets — i caught a
final glimpse of her agonized face eaten by caustic slime
— A scream faded out in birdcalls and jungle sounds and
lapping water —

July 14, 1962 — Present time — "i told you i would
come with tower fire — vomited the ghost food moved
noose — Four letters at dawn fell apart in 'havingness' —
muttering absent bodies hanged after being milked of
identities — Remember identities swirled through slow
motion all that links the green amphibious creature as they
rolled future time 1962 — I told you the skin underneath
flash bulbs was healed scars — male spirits trapped in
dead nitrous flesh — aroused courage to pass without doing picture — i saw now forgotten memory controlling
Game Hate Box — Opponents in green mummy get out
here — Donar popped — It is a grand feeling — Half-
healed scars peeling off these experiments between mutual erections — other flesh flapping through noose" —

"Just remember i was fish smells and absolute need —

condition empty but know the way to overwhelm — Flak holes told him khaki pants shifted ejaculating hostile land — flash of rectums naked in whiffs suddenly clicked to color — Invisible passenger took my skin off in sheets — burned like ice" —

"i told you i would come — Won't be much screen now — i have said basic time to go — Wind of morning disintegrates present time —"

*combat
troops in
the area*

As the shot of apomorphine cut through poisons of Minraud he felt a tingling burning numbness — his body coming out of deep freeze in the Ovens — Then viscera exploded in vomit — The mold of his body cracked and he stepped free — a slender green creature, his hands ended in black claws covered with fine magnetic wires that extended up the inner arm to the elbow — He was wearing a gas mask to breathe carbon dioxide of enemy planet — antennae ears tuned to all voices of the city, each voice classified on a silent switchboard — green disk eyes with pupils of a pale electric blue — body of a hard green substance like flexible jade — back brain and spine burned with blue sparks as messages crackled in and out —

"Shift body halves — Vibrate flesh — Cut tourists" —

The instructions were filed on transparent sheets waiting sound formation as he slid them into mind screens of the planet — He put on his broken body like an overcoat — Silent and purposeful under regulating center of the back brain, he went into a bar and stood at the pinball machine, his hard green core sinking into the other players writing the resistance message with magnetic wires — The machine clicked and tilted in his hands, electric purpose cutting association lines — Enemy plans exploded in a burst of rapid calculations — Vast insect calculating machine of the enemy flashed the warning —

"Combat troops in the area" —

Combat troops to fight the Insect People of Minraud for control of this planet — Crab guards gathered around the machine, sliding forward to feel with white-hot claws for the human spots of weakness opened up by The Green Boy of the Divide Line — The crab guard was not finding the spots — He pressed closer breathing the dry heat of Minraud, while flying scorpion men sank stingers into empty flesh, injecting the oven poison — Too late the crab guard saw the jade body and the disk eyes pounding deep into his nerve centers — The eyes converged in a single beam forcing the guard back like a fire hose — The pressure suddenly shut off as the eyes vibrated in air hammer synchronization — pounded the guard to writhing fragments —

The Scorpion Electricals buzzed away screaming — His converging eye beams exploded them in the air and they fell in a shower of blue sparks — He was standing over the green boy spitting words into his nervous system —

"Show me your controller — quickly or i kill" —

The green boy nodded — An old woman appeared on screen spitting phosphorescent hate, screaming for her shattered guard — the Lord of Time surrounded by files and calculating machines, word and image bank of a picture planet — It was over in a few stuttering seconds — Under vibrating pounding eyebeams that cut flesh and bone with electric needles her image blurred and exploded in a burst of nitrous film smoke — where she had stood a vast low-pressure area — winds of the earth through archives of Time as film and newspapers shredded to dust in a tornado of years and centuries —

"Word falling — Photo falling — Time falling — Break through in Grey Room" — Combat troops antennae crackling static orders poured inflexible violence along the middle line of body — took the planet in a few seconds cutting virus troops with stuttering light guns — galactic shock troops who never colonize — clicking tilting through pinball machines of the earth — lighting up the Board Books and dictating message of total resistance —

"Shift linguals — Cut word lines — Vibrate tourists — Free doorways — Pinball led streets — Word falling — Photo falling — Break through in Grey Room — Towers, open fire" —

Electric static orders poured through nerve circuits in stuttering seconds —

"Body halves off — appropriate instrument pinball color circuits — Sex words exploded in photo flash — Nitrous fumes drift from pinball machines and penny arcades of the world — Photo falling — Break through in grey room — Click, tilt, vibrate green goo planet — Towers, open fire — Explode word lines of the earth — Combat troops show board books and dictate out symbol language of virus enemy — Fight, controlled body prisoners

— Cut all tape — Vibrate board books with precise shared meals — scraps — remains of 'Love' from picture planet — Get up off your rotting combos lit up by a woman — Word falling — Free doorways — Television mind destroyed — Break through in Grey Room — 'Love' is falling — Sex word is falling — Break photograph — Shift body halves — Board books flashed idiot Mambo on 'their dogs' — with pale adolescents of love from Venus — Static orders pour in now — Venus camera writing all the things you are — Planet in 'Love' is a wind U turn back — Isn't time left — Partisans showing board books in Times Square in Piccadilly — Tune and sound effects vibrating sex whine along the middle line of body — Explode substitute planet — Static learned every board book symbol with inflexible violence — color writing you out of star dust — took board books written in prisoner bodies — cutting all tape — Love Mary? — picture planet — Its combos lit up a woman — 'Love' falling permutated through body halves — Static orders clicking — Word falling — Time falling — 'Love' falling — Flesh falling — Photo falling — Image falling" —

Controllers of the Green Troops moved in now — Light-years in eyes that write character of biologic alteration — Vampires fall to dust — crumpled cloth bodies on the glass and metal streets — The Venusians are relegated to terminal sewage deltas — The Uranians back to the heavy cold mist of mineral silence — Dry heat and insect forms close round the people of Mercury — Consequences and alternatives flash on off — Accept Rewrite or return to conditions you intended to impose on this colony — No appeal from eyes that see light-years in advance — Explode substitute giving orders — Green metal antennae crackling static in the transient hotels — cutting virus troops with static noises — Galactic shock troops break through moving in fast on music poured through nerve circuits — stuttering distant events — In a few seconds body halves off from St. Louis — Ghost writing shows board books — Vibrate dead nitrous film streets — Fight, controlled body prisoners — Cut flute through board books — Scraps to go, doctor — cleaving new planet — Get up, please — Television mind destroyed — Love is falling from this paper punching holes in photograph — Shift body halves in the womb — a long way from St. Louis — total resistance — cobblestone language with inflexible violence — Combat troops clicked the fair — a Barnum Bailey world — Word falling — Time falling — The fade-out — Good bye parasite invasion with weakness of dual structure, as the shot of apomorphine exploded the mold of their claws in vomit — Insect People Of Minraud preparing exact copy of scorpions crawling over his face — preparing exact copy of Bradly's body molded in two halves — Green boy slips the mold on during sex scene — Remember strange bed? mold heated up to 10,000 Fahrenheit — His street boy senses clicked an oven in transient flesh — Call in the Old Doctor — heavy twilight — A cigarette deal? — Kiki stepped forward —

"True? I can't feel it" —

"Yes, smiling" —

The man was only a face — Sex tingled in the shadow of street cafés — On the bed felt his cock stiffen — open fly — stroked it with gentle hands — Healed scars still pulsing in empty flesh of KY and rectal mucus — flicker

ghost only a few years older than Kiki — Outskirts of the
city, masturbated under thin pants — orgasms of memory
fingers — Blue twilight fell on his Scandinavian skin —
shadow beside him, KY on his slow fingers — As you
listen fill in with a pull — teeth ground together the
image track — Muscles relax and contract — Kicked his
feet in the air — steady stream of drum music in his head
— forgotten scent of pubic hairs in other flesh with loud
snores —

"Without you i on pavement — Saw a giant crab snapping — Help me — Sinking ship — You trying Ali God of
Street Boys on screen? — So we turn over knife wind
voices covered — From the radio interstellar sirocco" —

The room was full of white pillow flakes blowing out
from a conical insect nest of plaster — Scorpions crawled
from the nest snapping their claws — He felt the conical
nests attached to his side — white scorpions crawling over
his face — He woke up screaming: "Take them off me —
Take them off me" —

The dream still shuddered in milky dawn light — Kiki
lay naked in a strange bed — His street boy senses clicked
back: standing in a doorway his collar turned up against
the cold Spring wind that whistled down from the moun-
tains — The man stopped under a blue arc light in the
heavy twilight — He put a cigarette to his mouth, tapped
his pockets, and turned his hands out — Kiki stepped forward with his lighter extended smiling — The man was
only a few years older than Kiki — thin face hidden by
the shadow of his hat — They had sandwiches and beer
at a booth where a kerosene lamp flickered in the mountain wind — The man called a cab that seemed to leave

the ground on a long ride through rubbly outskirts of the city — It was a neighborhood of large houses with gardens — In the apartment Kiki sat down on the bed and felt his cock stiffen under thin pants as the man stroked it with gentle abstract fingers — Blue twilight fell through the room — He could only see a shadow beside him — Kiki took the man's hand and closed the fist and shoved a finger in and out —

"I fuck you?" —

"*Sí*" —

The man put on a tape of Arab drum music — Kiki had been a week in the cold streets dodging the police who were everywhere checking papers after the manner of their species — He dropped his worn pants and stood naked — His cock slid out of the foreskin pulsing — As he sat down again on the bed a drop of lubricant squeezed out and glistened in the faint bluish light — The man sat down beside him and kissed him feeling his cock — Kiki pushed the man back on the bed — He found a tube of KY on the night table — On his knees above the dark shadowy figure he rubbed the KY on his cock — He put his hands under the man's knees and shoved them up to the ears and rubbed the KY into the man's ass with a slow circular pull — Teeth ground together as Kiki slid his cock in feeling the muscle relax and contract in spasmodic milking movements — The man kicked his feet in the air — "*Juntos*" said Kiki — He began to count and at the count of ten they came together — Kiki fell into a light sleep the drum music in his head — He woke up to find the man lighting a candle — "Cigarette?" — The man brought a package of cigarettes and lay down beside him

— Kiki blew the smoke down through his pubic hairs and said "Abracadabra" as his cock rose out of the smoke — He rolled the man over, then pulled him up onto his knees and fucked him to the music — He draped himself over the man's back with loud snores — He was in fact very tired after the street, yawned as he crawled under the covers and snuggled against the man's back —

The man was not in bed beside him but seated at a table crumpled forward his head sunk into the collar of a heavy silk dressing gown — A muffled sound like muttering cloth drifted from the crumpled form — Kiki got out of bed naked and touched the man's shoulder — There was nothing there but cloth that fell in a heap on the floor leaking grey dust — Kiki found the man's wallet and slipped out the large bills — The man's clothes were too large so he put on his own clothes and went out shutting the door softly — He listened for a moment then stepped quickly down the stairs — In the doorway he stumbled over a pile of rags that smelled of urine and pulque — empty streets and from radios in empty houses a twanging sound of sirens that rose and fell vibrating the windows — The air was full of luminous grey flakes falling softly on crumpled cloth bodies — The street led to an open square — He could see people running now suddenly collapse to a heap of clothes — The grey flakes were falling heavier, falling through all the buildings of the city — Cold fear touched his street boy senses — A vista of phosphorescent slag heaps opened before him —

On the smoldering metal he saw a giant crab claws snapping — A voice in Kiki's head said "Stand aside" as Ali God of Street Boys from the neon cities of Saturn moved in — Dodging from side to side over the snapping claws his plasma knife tore a great rent in the crab's body that leaked black rusty oil — Ali doubled back from above and behind hitting the crab at the base of its brain — The claws flew off — The eyes went out — There was nothing but a smear of oil on the pavement —

"This way — To the Towers" — Ali pointed to an office building that dominated the square — Kiki ran toward the building covered now by tower fire — Hands pulled him into a doorway — On the roof of the building was a battery of radios and movie cameras that vibrated to static — A green creature with metal claw hands was giving orders to a group of partisans who manned the gun tower — From the radio poured a metallic staccato voice —

"Photo falling — Word Falling — Break through in Grey Room — Towers, open fire" —

Totally green troops in the area, K9 — You are assigned to organize combat divisions at the Venusian Front — appalling conditions — total weapons — Without inoculation and training your troops will be paralyzed by enemy virus and drugs — then cut to pieces in the pain-pleasure signal switch — The enemy uses a vast mechanical brain to dictate the use and rotation of weapons — Precise information from virus invasion marks areas of weakness in the host and automatically brings into effect the weapons and methods of attack calculated always of course with alternate moves — They can turn on total pain of the Ovens — This is done by film and brain wave recordings mangled down to a form of concrete music — A twanging sound very much like positive feedback correlated with the Blazing Photo from Hiroshima and Nagasaki — They can switch on electric pleasure leading to death in orgasm — (The noose is a weapon — The weapon of Kali) — They can alternate pain and pleasure at supersonic speed like a speed up tough and con cop routine —

You are to infiltrate, sabotage and cut communications — Once machine lines are cut the enemy is helpless — They depend on elaborate installations difficult to move or conceal — encephalographic and calculating machines film and TV studios, batteries of tape recorders — Remember you do not have to organize similar installations but merely to put enemy installations out of action or take them over — A camera and two tape recorders can cut the lines laid down by a fully equipped film studio — The ovens and the orgasm death tune in can be blocked with large doses of apomorphine which breaks the circuit of positive feedback — But do not rely too heavily on this protection agent — They are moving to block apomorphine by correlation with nausea gas that is by increasing the nausea potential — And always remember that you are operating under conditions of guerrilla war — Never attempt to hold a position under massive counterattack — "Enemy advance we retreat" — Where? — The operation of retreat on this level involves shifting three-dimensional coordinate points that is time travel on association lines — Like this:

sunlight through the dusty window and sat down on the sofa the pearly drops of the basement workshop . . "You're pearling." flaking plaster . . you finish me John's face grey and whispy spurts of semen across off ". . long

ago boy a soft blue flame in the dusty floor the static still
in image speed of light his eyes as he bent over his ears
rose shadows on the ten years the pool hall the crystal
radio set young flesh . ." John is it true on Market St. Bill
leaned touching dials and "if we were ten light-years
away we across the table and wires with gentle precise
fingers could see ourselves here John goosed him with
"I'm trying to fix it so we can both ten years from now?
a cue and he collapsed listen at once." "Yes it's true."
"Well couldn't we across the table laughing . . he was
opening a headphone on the bench travel in time?" they
had not seen much with a screwdriver . . "It's more complicated than you think." of each other in the two heads so
close John's "well time is past ten years . . Bill had been
fluffy blond hair brushed Bill's getting dressed and away
at school and later forehead. undressed eating sleeping not the Eastern University. John had "Here hold this
phone to your ear" actions but the words became a legendary figure Do you hear anything?" "What we say about
what we living by gambling . . he used "yes static." do.
Would there be any time if systems for dice and horses
based on "Good" John cupped the other phone we didn't
say a mathematical theories . . to his ear. anything?"
"Maybe not. Maybe that St. Louis summer night outside
smell the two boys at poised listening coal gas the
moon red and out through the dusty window first step"
smoky . . they walked through empty across back yards
and ash pits . . "Yes if you could learn park frogs croaking"
"John the tinkling metal music of space to listen and not
lived in a loft over a Bill felt a prickle in his lips talk" . .
over the hills and speak-easy reached by that spread to

the groin. far away . . sunlight through outside wooden stairs . . sunlight through the dusty window of the basement workshop John's face grey wispy a soft blue flame in his eyes as he bent over the crystal radio set touching dials and wires with gentle precise fingers.

"I'm trying to fix it so we can both listen at once."

He was opening a headphone on the bench with a screwdriver the two heads so close John's fluffy blond hair brushed Bill's forehead.

"Here hold this phone to your ear. Do you hear anything?"

"Yes static."

"Good."

John cupped the other phone to his ear. The two boys sat poised listening out through the dusty window across back yards and ash pits the tinkling metal music of space. Bill felt a prickle in his lips that spread to the groin. He shifted on the wooden stool.

"John what is static exactly?"

"I've told you ten times. What's the use in my talking when you don't listen?"

"I hear music" . . faint intermittent 'Smiles.' Bill moving in time to the music brushed John's knee . . "Let's do it shall we?"

"All right"

John put the headphones down on the bench. There was a storage room next to the work shop. Bill opened the door with a key. He was the only one who had this key. smell of musty furniture . . smears of phosphorous paste on the walls . . Bill turned on a lamp a parchment shade with painted roses . . chairs upside down on a desk a leather sofa cracked and shiny. The boys stripped to their socks and sat down on the sofa.

"You're pearling."
spurts of semen across the dusty floor static still in his ears rose shadows on young flesh . .

"John is it true if we were ten light-years away we could see ourselves here ten years from now?"

"Yes it's true."

"Well couldn't we travel in time?"

"It's more complicated than you think."

"Well time is getting dressed and undressed eating sleeping not the actions but the *words* . . What we *say* about what we do. Would there be any time if we didn't say anything?"

"Maybe not. Maybe that would be the first step . . yes if we could learn to listen and not talk."

Over the hills and far away sunlight through the dusty window a soft blue flame in his eyes as he bent over . . his ears rose shadows on the crystal radio set . . He shifted on the wood the dusty window . . "Come up for a while" he said . . stool semen on the sofa a soft blue flame in "All right" Bill felt a tightening "John what is static exactly?" his eyes as he bent over in his stomach . . it was a room "I've told you ten times what his ears rose shadows on with rose wallpaper use of my saying anything. the crystal radio set partitioned off like a stage set when you don't listen?" . . "I'm trying to fix it so we can both . . Bill saw a work 'I hear music' ten years from now listen at once" he was bench tools and radio faint intermittent 'Smiles' . . opening travel in time sets from the light John Bill moving in time to the with a screwdriver" hold this turned on . .

the music brushed John's knee. phone to your ear the words do you door he had painted Bill turned to John smiling hear anything? . . we didn't say to his ear a number like "Let's do it shall we?" anything maybe not maybe the two hotel door No. "All right" boys poised listening out through 18 . . "Sit down" John took out a John put down the headphones on the dusty window would cigarette from a box on the bench. be the first step across back yards and ash pits the night table there was storage room next to the yes if you could it was rolled in brown work- shop. Bill opened learn the tinkling metal music of space paper . . "What is it?" the door with a key . . "That static gave me a hard-on." "Marijuana . . ever try it" "No" he was the only one who had like something touched me he lit the cigarette and the key. The smell and he brought his finger up . . passed to Bill "Take it all musty furniture smears in three jerks sitting with their the way down and hold phosphorous paste on the walls arms around each other's that's right . ." Bill Bill turned on a lamp parchment shoulders looking down at feet a prickling in his shade with painted roses the stiffening flesh flower smell lips . . the wallpaper chairs upside down on a desk of young hard-ons "Let's see who can seemed to glow leather sofa cracked and shiny shoot the farthest" then he was laughing the boys stripped to their socks they stood up Bill hit the wall until he doubled "I'm trying to fix it so we can both ten years from now listen at once." opening travel in time with a screwdriver "Hold this phone to your ear. the words Do you hear anything?" We didn't say to his ear anything maybe not maybe the two boys poised listen- ing out through the dusty window would be the first step across back yards and ash pits yes if you could learn the tinkling metal music of space "That static gave me a hard-on like something touched me" he brought his finger up in three jerks sitting with arms around each other's shoulders looking down at the stiffening flesh flower smell of young hard-ons

"Let's see who can shoot the farthest."

They stood up. Bill hit the wall . . the pearly drops . . flaking plaster . .

"you finish me off" . . .

long ago boy image . . speed of light . . ten years . . the pool hall on Market St . . Bill leaned across the table for a shot and John goosed him with a cue he collapsed across the table laughing. They had not seen much of each other in the past ten years. Bill had been away at school and later at an Eastern University. John had become a legendary figure around town who lived by gambling he used a system for dice and horses based on a mathematical theory which accounted for the only constant factor in gambling: winning and losing comes in streaks. So double up when you are winning and fold up when you are losing . . St. Louis summer night outside the pool hall smell of coal gas the moon red they walked through an empty park frogs croaking John lived over a speak-easy by the river . . a loft reached by outside wooden stairs.

"Come up for a while," he said

"All right." Bill felt a tightening in his stomach. A room with rose wallpaper had been partitioned off from the loft like a stage set. As John turned on the light Bill saw a work bench tools and radio sets in the loft. On the door to the bedroom John had painted a number like a hotel door No 18 . .

"Sit down" . . John took a cigarette from a box on the night table. It was rolled in brown paper.

"What is it?"

"Marijuana. Ever try it?"

"No" . . John lit the cigarette and passed it to Bill. "Take it all the way down and hold it . . That's right . ."

Bill felt a prickling in his lips. The wallpaper seemed to glow. Then he was laughing doubled over on the bed laughing until it hurt his ribs laughing. "My God I've pissed in my pants."

(Recollect in the officers' club Calcutta Mike and me was high on Ganja laughed till we pissed all over ourselves and the steward said "You bloody hash heads get out of here.")

He stood up his grey flannel pants stained down the left leg sharp odor of urine in the hot St. Louis night.

"Take them off I can lend you a pair."

Bill kicked off his moccasins. Hands on his belt he hesitated.

"John I uh . ."

"Well so what?"

"All right." Bill dropped his pants and shorts.

"Your dick is getting hard . . . Sit here." John patted the bed beside him.

Bill tossed his shirt onto a chair. He stretched his legs out and knocked his feet together.

John tossed his shirt onto the floor by the window. He stood up and dropped his pants. He was wearing red shorts. He pulled his shorts down scraping erection and dropped the shorts over the lamp testing the heat with his hands. "All right," he decided his gentle precise fingers on Bill's shoulder fold sweet ecetera to bed — EE Cummings if my memory serves and what have I my friend to give you? Monkey bones of eddie and bill? John's shirt in the dawn light? . . dawn sleep . . smell of late morning in the room? Sad old human papers I carry . . empty magic of young nights . . Now listen . . ugh . . the dust the bribe . . (precise finger touching dead old path) . . was a window . . you . . ten-year-old face of laughter . . was a window of laughter shook the valley . . sunlight in his eyes for an instant Johnny's figure shone to your sudden "do it" . . stain on the sheets . . smell of young nights . .

vaudeville
voices

    Clinic outside East St. Louis on stilts over the wide brown river took in a steady stream of distant events — That week they could stay on the nod — time there after a rumble in Dallas — Music runs back to the '20s — Ten-year-old keeping watch — cracked pavements — sharp scent of weeds that grow in suburbs — pool hall and vaudeville voices —

    So we turn over steady stream of distant events and we flush out traces of a time that meanwhile i had forgotten — wet air thick and dirty on the garage — sharp scent of memory pictures coming in — Looked for him he was gone — I met everybody in deserted cemetery with wooden crosses — There was a mulatto about —

"True? — i can't feel it — Yes you have his face — healed and half-healed skin — Put it on — Without you i on pavement — perhaps if you had helped me — Good bye then — That silver film took it away from me — Well fade-out" —

Trails my Summer dawn wind in other flesh strung together on scar impressions of young Panama night — Pictures exploded in the kerosene lamp spattered light on naked rectum open shirt flapping in the pissoir — Cock flipped out and up — water from his face — The street blew rain from spurts of his crotch — Young faces melted to musical clock hands and brown ankles — dead nitrous streets — fish smell in doorways —

Look at the wired electric maze of the city — Stop — No good — Wait a bit — the long mat — It was an errand boy from the death trauma — The boy who entered the '20s had his own train — Room in the half-light source of second wind spread the difference between life and death — Boneless mummy was death in the last round —

So we turn over what he did not know: Window people and sky pictures fade out at dawn — Hurry up — Hands crowd — In the tremendous flash your brain splintered on empty flesh — bleeding boneless panting death in the last round — the gate from darkened eyes of wine still loaded with physical skin — Put it on?? *End Of The Line* —

Remember i was fish smell and dead eyes in doorway — errand boy from last stroke of nine — room in the half-light beside you — Great wind voices of Alamout it's you? — My duty has been remitted muttering: "Not think any more of your harsh thoughts" — But who am i to say more? — Empty is the third in vacant lot — Duty remitted — Sound of fear and i dance — crumpled cloth bodies empty — ash from falling tracks — open shirt flapping wind from the South — the throat designed to water — I stay near the basin and shadow pools — Invisible man on webs of silver cut tracks — Vapor trails writing the sky of Alamout and back i shall go — indications enough in the harbor — muttering of dry rivers — fish smell and dead eyes in doorways — The sirocco dances to sound of the crowds — harsh at this time of day — vultures in the street — Know the answer? — Around in vacant lot 1910 — weeds growing through broken towers — His face screen went dead — smell of healed and half-healed scars — silver film at the exits — Won't be much left — Little time so I'll say: "Good night" — not looking around — talking away — of distant events in green neon — You touched from frayed jacket — improvised shacks — mufflers — small pistols — quick fires from bits of driftwood — Shadow voices muttering in the dog rotation — Acoustic qualities couldn't reach flesh — between suns desolate underbrush — sharp scent of weeds that grow in old Westerns — battered phonograph talking distant events — Important thing is always courage to pass without stopping —

Naked boy on association line — i stay near right now — be shifted harsh at this time of day — The levanto dances between mutual erections fading in hand — trails my Summer afternoons — Slow fingers in dawn sleep tore the flesh from words — fish smell and dead train whistles — open shirt flapping — wind of morning in the harbor — My number is K9 — I am a Biologic from frayed jacket sitting out in lawn chairs with the St. Louis suburb — not looking around — talking away — arab drum music in the suburban air — fading khaki pants as we shifted this pubescent flesh murmur of human nights like death in your throat? — breathless — my name — faded through the soccer scores. Tuesday was the last day for signing years . . July 7 St Auberge — (ambiguous sign of an inn) . . stand in for Mr *Who*?? My name was called like this before rioters bleed without return . . *We want to hear pay talk dad and we want to hear pay talk now* . . Yes that's me still there waiting in the empty Tangier street . . sunshine and shadow of Mexico . . a night in Madrid . . You let this happen?? (holding the laser gun in his hands) . . wrecked markets half-buried in sand . . smell of blood and excrement in the Tangier streets . . ("We wont be needing you after Friday returning herewith Title Insurance Policy No.17497.") . . You don't remember me? showing you the papers I carry . . diseased bent over burnt-out inside . . coordinates gangrene . . Hiroshima gangrene . . "Frankly doctor we don't like to hear the word 'nova' here . . bringing you the Voice of American . . This is November 18, 1963 . . This is Independence Day in Morocco . . The Independence is in the harbor of Tangier . . The Independence is an *American* boat . . The *American* Independence is in Morocco . . This is Independence Day in Morocco . . This is *American* Independence Day in Morocco . . This is July 4, 1964 in Morocco . . Brook's Park . . the old swimming pool kinda run down now . . Mack the Knife over the loudspeaker . . (He has loosed the fatal lightning of his terrible swift sword) . . Ghostly looking child burned a hole in the blanket . . brief flight to Gib . . Our business now has no future

. . know human limitations? Captain Clark welcomes you aboard . . Remember show price? — (holding the gun in his hands) . . You don't remember this sad stranger there on the sea wall wishing you luck from dying lips? And remember the 'Priest' . . They called him and he stayed . . (boat whistling in the harbor) . . Well that's about the closest way I know to tell you and papers rustling across city desks . . fresh southerly winds a long time ago . . going through the files like this . . agony to breathe in sad muttering voices . .

"Now how's this for an angle, B.J.? *a real American* stand . . Everything America ever stood for in any man's dream America stands for now . . Everything this country could have been and wasn't it will be now . . Every promise America ever made America will redeem now . ."
agony to breathe in the Boy's Magazine . . as I have told you sad guards remote posts . . came to a street half-buried in sand . . transitory halting place in this mutilated phantom . . smell of strange parks . . shabby quarters of a forgotten city . . his cold distant umbrella to the harbor office . . last intersection there smell of ashes . . tin can flash flare . . wind stirs a lock of hair . . a young man waiting . . hockshop kid like mother used to make . . distant hand lifted sad as his voice . . "quiet now . . I go . ." (flickering silver smile) . .

"A militant writer's union . . All American writers recalled to base . . Stand by for orders . . All you jokers in the Shakespeare Squadron return to base immediately and stand by for orders . ."

The Frisco Kid he never returns . . in life used address I gave you for that belated morning . . agony to breathe in this mutilated phantom . . last intersection dim jerky far away voice . .

"It's the greatest story conference in history, B.J. . . . All these writers assembled in the warehouse of the Atlantic Tea Company . . These writers are going to *write history as it happens in present time* . . And I don't want to hear any Banshee wails from you skypilots . . Now the way I see it is this: *America stands for doing the job* and that's what's wrong with America today . . half-assed assassins . . half-assed writers . . half-assed plumbers . . a million actors . . one corny part . . So we write a darned good part for every actor on the American set . . You gotta see the whole scene as a *show* . ."

"Remember show price? Know who I am? . . . 'Good Bye Mister' is my name . . . 'Wind and Dust' is my name . . 'Never Happened' is my name . . ."

Soccer scores — The driver shrugged — His sound i could describe to the open street car passing whiffs of Spain — long empty face — his eyes the evening breeze where the awning flapped — Violence roared past the Café de France cleaving a heavy summons — Mr Bradly, hurry up — Wind Ariel closed your account — Hurry up please its street — harbor lights gently moving water smiles dimmer at the edges — arab memory of flesh far now — Such people made a wide U turn back to the '20s —

Totally green troops in the area — We come to shape the five new combat divisions through clear process in the United States — slow your brain area trade — Impressions of present time played electrical music — Faded guards blew red nitrous fumes over you — khaki pants fully understood all of idiot Mambo spattered to control mechanization — hot sex words crackling paper and punching holes in it —

rectums naked in whiffs of raw meat — Jissom fell languidly bare feet afternoons — a Mexican about twenty shifting Johnny's knees — He was in the room on genital smells finger shared meals and belches — feeling like scenic railways in sleep — suitcases all open — on association line electric spasms — burning outskirts of the city — dark street life of a place forgotten —

Invisible passenger took my hands in dawn sleep of water music — Broken towers intersect cigarette smoke memory of each other — healed hands like ice — Won't be much — Screen went dead — He dressed hastily shirt flapping — stared out from darkened eyes of wine gas —

"Good bye then — I thought" — He walked through dawn mirror of Panama — Memory hit spine outside 1920 movie theater — sat down open shirts flapping — Many did not listen — silver film at the exits — *Weilest du?* — dead nitrous flesh — dirty look through glass — Who is that naked corpse? — Come along ladies and gentlemen — screaming on the deal in many lips? — She didn't get it — Cut the image like back in the restaurant — Wait a bit — No good — half-healed electric needs — dead scars — Leave him to me — Won't be much left — For a room in the shoeshine boy Swedish river of Gothenberg? — Release without more ado what? — When i left you hear little tune cut the image —

"i am surrounded through cafés and restaurants — Rabble rousers fade in coffee cup reflections — Blood? — There is no Jewish blood flash scarlet invitations to young

anti-Semites — Tourist as all the Jewish people i see myself impoverished tired hustler — Anti-Semite is buried
forever in my deferential nods — Today i am as old in
years as flapping human genitals in Mexico — i am surrounded — bodies and water everywhere — Blood runs
in the pale door — My early rabble rousers give off a
stench of rotten lips departed — nothing here — wind
voices" —

terminal
street

"Bradly passed through the twisting intestinal streets
— terminal streets of Minraud — A boy of dead nitrous
flesh wafted from a doorway of tarnished silver —

"Me good sewage and frozen jissom — beautiful
peoples" —

They talk in clouds of scent from glands in the groin.
— A whiff of KY and rectal mucus drifted out in propositions of memory orgasm — scent talk of dead film people
— terminal guide here, Mister — He made of 1920 movie
— In a vacant lot a scorpion boy was eating a pile of
metal excrement — He peered up at Bradly from phosphorescent glittering eyes —

"Me good guide, Meester — Here very bad peoples" —
The boy vibrated his stinger — "Very bad peoples — So
you fucked, Johnny" —

They moved through paths in a vast rubbish heap —
Came to a cliff city that towered out of sight in the hot
blue sky — cubicles connected by catwalks and ladders

and platforms — The guide moved on music currents waiting for the beats and chords that lifted them up ladders and ramps, swept them along perilous platforms over voids of billowing heat —

"You learn quick, Meester — Music talk — In here" —

They clicked through melodious turnstiles — The walls glowed with slow metal fires — Music currents swirled through the room — The guide twisted out of his scorpion shell — a being two feet tall covered by fine red hairs that vibrated in puffs of nitrous smoke — His head converged to a sharp beak — The penis of black gristle was covered with the fine red hairs except for the naked tip which came to a quivering point —

"We fuck now — Then i taking you to the Elder — Very old — Very wise — You see" — Bradly took off his space suit and lay down on a pallet that pulsed to sex music — The fine red hairs penetrated his pores — His body dissolved in a choking erogenous mist of burning sex films — The pointed penis penetrated his rectum — He ejaculated spurts of red smoke —

"Now we going to the Elder — He *inside* — Never come out" —

Came to a round metal chamber lined with switchboards and view screens — Embedded in a limestone dais was a grey foetal dwarf, his brain clearly visible under a thin membrane pulsed with colored lights as he controlled the switchboard —

"He make all music," said the guide —

The dwarf turned his eyeless face to Bradly — Bradly could feel radar beams map his outlines — Words passed through his mind on silver ticker tape —

"No one of your race has ever been here before — As a visitor you are disastrous — That is why i attempted to block you — When i did not succeed i knew of course that our blockade was broken by intervention from the Saturn Galaxy — Now it seems we must submit to basic alterations — We do not have 'emotions oxygen' in our atmosphere — The heat here kills what you call 'emotion' — That is where centipedes and scorpions come from — a heat that kills emotion and animates a bundle of nerve wires — Very few were able to survive here and those few paid the price of specialization" —

Last controls fade out at dawn — young faces moving absent bodies — empty source of second suit — open shirt in the dim light — Ejaculated skin back into dying forms — the face a picture — people gone —

"Me good guide, Meester" — suffused a time that i had street boy head) —

"i take you see all Garden Delights" —

Boys hang from gallows, turn flapping against each other — dissolved in smoke and crumpled cloth — guided by metal music the doctor on stage —

"i told you i would cover being of healed scars — The doctor still am the Big Fix" —

The whole being suddenly shut off in puffs of nitrous smoke — music cure last parasite — The face was broken — Do not have slow-motion flashes — Dying forms overtake "Mr Bradly Mr Martin" — moving slowly out of the sick lies — No trying source of second rectum tape — smell of empty condoms in the dim light — brain of Gothenberg moved on at dawn — bread knife currents — the cold *adios* without a shadow — here caught in the door

— no shelter — A street boy's head questions board room breath trade — Glittering eyes peered up and: "Man, like good bye" — Ding dong bell — Silence — Solitude — Bradly leaning say: "Good bye then in currents waiting for the carbon dioxide — Truly *adiós*" — Bitter price — Martin is like pulp behind —

A prospect of red mesas rising from blue depths — Suspended over the void a precarious iron city of cable cars, elevators, ferris wheels, scenic railways and plane rides all in constant motion — "Here" said the guide and clicked Bradly into a cubicle that permutated through the structure, floating in slow vertigo of ferris wheels, clicking along perilous tracks where wind whistled through the cables — The guide turned up his eyes like a blue torch cutting along the divide line of Bradly's naked body — Electric needle fingers removed his skin, pulling it loose in red sheets of pain hung it on a peg — The guide slipped off his own skin like a garment, peeled penis pulsing red light, clouds drifting through his remote blue eyes — Hula hoops of color formed around the guide's body and enclosed Bradly weak and torn with pain cool hands on his naked flesh as he sank in blood and bones and intestines of the other suffocation panic of spermatozoa sucked through pearly genital passages and spurted out in a scratching shower of sperm — sunlight through bodies without cover — soft luminous spurts drifting in the cold blue wind —

Body tension in genital rings and he fell into the explosion of sperm — Contraction turnstiles ejaculated bodies without cover — Iridescent orgasm floated from pale adolescents — Slow movement of body hairs ejaculated

the creature who talks in color blast — iridescent weak
and torn by pain, decay breathing from years spurting
out through the orgasm death in black lust of the swamp
mud — black fish movement of food, intestines shifting
color orgasm reflected in the obsidian penis — Silver films
in the blood and bones tear his insides apart — He was
sucked from penis suffocation and released dream flesh in
a scratching shower of sperm — sunlight through pubic
hairs — soft luminous spurts of memory riding the wind
— Pieces of cloud drifted through someone walking —
Mountain wind around his body trailing sweat drew him
into other body alterations, sky blue through viscera of
the other — solitude of morning cool on his skinned
flesh —

last
round over

Now for me — the story of one White — That's why
darkies were born — way human skin inflated "Master"
— a long good night in metal valve at base of the spine —
now for the story of one absent today far from the old
folks — softly singing Old Black Joe to "music" (i made an
ambiguous gesture) of cold crystal grave — ghost rectums
of cotton — Semen fell like opal cane — Weep no more —
absent tenants — silence to say good bye *adiós* — controllers from the ancient white planet of frozen gasses —
a vast mineral consciousness near absolute zero thinking
in slow formations of crystal — silent female navigators
blank space eyes swept by Northern Lights — yeti men

with burning metal eyes and long claws covered with purple hair shock troops carried by the navigators — controllers of the White Smoke and the utilities, monopolized and froze the earth — The White Smoke and the White Light keeps the Djoun forces away and in darkness they assume malignant forms — So you need the White Light to keep them away —

"It's the old junk gimmick — Freeze the mark — Thawing hurts you got it? — Sex and pain forms hatching out in paralyzed flesh — and hatching out hungry — so you need more and more of the white stuff to keep your ass in deep freeze — Junk is not blue and it is not green — Junk is *White White White* — like the colorless no-smell of death from kicking addicts — That's where they get the White Smoke, from sick addicts — bottled in precinct cells of America — in Lexington, Kentucky — You got it? — Sex and pain *form* flesh identity" —

At far end pale flesh blooms slowly out of a life cannot exist in pictures — bleeding formations of crystal — that body without a shadow without relics — blank face, healed and half-healed dream flesh hatching from the death trauma — outside East St. Louis a cold *adiós* — silence — weary — They tell you of distant coffin — Won't be much left on Panama night — empty condom ticket — erogenous cotton flesh lying there streaked with phosphorous — someone walking —

"Man, like good bye then" —

(In the lunar caves black newt boys, eyes lips and genitals glowing with slow metal fires — penis rose in a smell of phosphorus — blue radium symbols on the wall) —

Now explosions of Colored South from mixture —

surges of silence from long metal night weaves people
and sky story of one absent today — on a slow boat to
China, Master, a long good night — the cold *adiós* —
Got no home? — So we'll sing one song: a big bank roll
and Cousin Miranda making a Monday line — So we'll
sing one song in your dreams — And that heart grows
weary — They'll tell you of money in the cold cold grave?
— on a slow boat to China, *adiós* — keeps on rolling a big
word line — sugar line — secondhand erogenous corn —
softly singing Old Black Joe to: "i'm tired of you and i'm
checking out" — Just to raise the price of a ticket angle
voices calling Old Black Joe — orgasm death in the cold
empty condom — Look, Master, God's wind blew icicles
in black slow-motion faces — singing phosphorus in flash
darkies weeping — broken glaciers and skin of cotton —
Weep no more — absent tenants — ghost voices calling
false human hosts — (i made an ambiguous gesture) —
Cold crystal semen fell like opal cane — slow motion sky
swept by Northern lights — Thawing hurts — White form
hatching in painted human skin inflated "Master" — long
hunger of the spine — Story of your ass in deep freeze? —
Semen fell like opal canes from phallic statues of ice under
Northern Lights — the cold of interstellar space in his
spine — sex and pain explosions of colored flesh hatching
out — That's why darkies were born — way the White
Stuff keep "Master" — Colorless Utilities monopolized
land of the free — Keeps the Djoun forces in secondhand
erogenous corn — So you need more and more of death
because your ass is in deep freeze — White White White
spurted again and again from death of kicking addicts —
need the White Light to check out — It's the old gim-

mick — Darkies are the pipes you got it? — sex and pain price of a ticket — flesh hatching out in cotton-covered orgasm cocoons —

(The ship came apart here like a rotten undervest — The yeti thawed to stings of white-hot scorpion people in the Ovens — Blasted his way out white sheets dripping purple fire — metal eyes burning in nova) —

Earthquakes and hurricanes exploded setup of mineral dreamer — space eyes blank as polar moon of morning — The question caught our ticket that exploded — need the White Smoke to circumstance — Remember i was the door — It's the old naked dream beside you — You got sex and pain information? — mouth of hair? —

(An orchid with brilliant red and green flowers hanging over the swamp mud — As i touched the plant long tendrils covered with fine erectile hairs stung my naked body, liquid fires feeling into mouth and penis and rectum) —

ancient evil odors on the trade winds — bottled female smells in corridors of silence —

"We intersect on empty kingdom where picture cannot exist — Bleeding i made this dream five times without a shadow without relics in the last terrace of the garden — Sex dawn and dream flesh left no address — For i have known East St. Louis good night — Isn't time is there left? — So we'll sing a song in white to give you — odor of deluge and money in dreams — Distant coffin overtakes me — bitter darkies caught in the door — ordor of drowned suns — Cold empty condom the price on our ticket that exploded — Any case divide line melted before circumstances — Remember i was the cotton flesh lying there — icicles at the far end of evening — broken dream beside you and the dreamer gone — with dirty shirt boy's lips fading out — Dark body smell filled the cave of dust — We made it all in spurts of burning phosphorous — on the walls slow radium circumstances — You can say could give no flesh identity — fading such words — What have i my friend to give? — pale roots where flesh blooms slowly out of life i led — read formations of crystal — Healed and half-healed shade departed from the death trauma — outside the body of a God bending cold *adiós* — Bitter, my friend, weary they tell you of courage to let go — Someone walking stopped suddenly to question cold grave — The pipes are calling Panama alterations — someone walking and we drown — erogenous naked flesh empty in the trade winds at dawn whisper — Man, like good bye" —

A young man of high condition gives you phosphorescent eyes and lips — lunar knife welded into his twisting shadow — phosphorescent dust tracing a colorless dreamer — wrote explosion of dawn and dream — ebbing night far from shirt in another — stopped suddenly to crown a God bending the cold *adiós* back to mineral silence — a big bank roll and Cousin Miranda falling — odor of no home — Silver flakes closed your account — recorder music in the throat of God — Won't be much left on the mirrors — empty tape — 1920 movie — Erogenous dust falls from demagnetized patterns — Rectums dissolve in blue dawn explosions of color sky — old Westerns rotting through slate music and nitrous fumes — Light layers peel off story of one absent today —spectral smell of empty condoms down along penny arcades and mirrors — silence to say good bye —

Now rewrite Mr Bradly Mr Martin — The separation gimmick that keeps this tired old show on the road — i have said Martin's life line is the human addict — That is why he is at such pains to keep the addict uncomfortably short — It is the need, the colorless death smell arising from sick addicts that keep his whole universe of junk time and monopoly in operation — "the White Smoke" bottled in precinct cells of America, in Lexington, Kentucky — With "the White Smoke" in one hand and "the Blue Heavy Metal Fix" in the other he has human hosts the way he likes to see them: caught in the switch — And if they make it out of that switch the Garden of Delights is there waiting with "Orgasm Death" — Make it out of there? — "the Ovens" down in the hole — All right, so you sewed up a planet — Now unsew it — Is that clear enough or shall i make it even clearer ? ? — Reverse all your gimmicks — your heavy blue metal fix out in blue sky — your blue mist swirling through all the streets of image to Pan Pipes — your white smoke falling in luminous sound and image flakes — your bank of word and image scattered to the winds of morning — into this project all the way or all to see in Times Square in Piccadilly — Reverse and dismantle your machine — Drain off the prop ocean and leave the White Whale stranded — all your word line broken from mind screens of the earth — You talk about "responsibility" — Now show responsibility — Show total responsibility — You have blighted a planet — Now remove the blight — Cancel your "White Smoke" and all your other gimmicks of control — your monopoly of life, time, and fortune canceled by your own orders — Pay, Mr Bradly Mr Martin — wracked and answer a God melted the recorders — out of the sick lies — no rectum tape — empty music cross the water — Characters walk in and out of silver film — smoke words recorded on scar impressions — Permutating the door, Mr Martin — A hand scattered word and image to the winds for all to see — Ding-dong bell — Silence — Mr Bradly Mr Martin, leaning say:

"Good bye then — Your machine drains off picture dioxide — Truly *adiós*" —

bitter price — whale stranded — the colors released, Martin is like pulp behind — Now remove all your gimmicks in setting forth — This dream be your orders — Your ticket now ended — All Martin's recorded speech fade-out — Mr Bradly Mr Martin, now show blighted planet the dog tape empty of control —

"Man, like vaudeville voices under the story" —

"Mirrors of Mr Bradly Mr Martin — calm his face — dream shut off — I fold the Old Doctor twice — in the gutter cosmic dust of nova — outside East St. Louis last good bye — memory pictures — the story over — back to invisible shadow — Yes you have bitter indications enough in empty room — someone walking — truly good bye then in Summer dawn wind — saucers in the morning sky — silence of the sick lies — 'Marks?' —Identity melted before daybreak — Like little time in tarnished offices — splintered on empty flesh — evening finger fading — God Of Panic talking" —

"Like good bye then, Willy the Rat — Remember i was the dreamer with dirty flesh — known end of the line outside 1920 movie streaked with violence — Film flakes drift *adiós* — Showed you your air — The Doctor on stage

— The pipes are calling — September left no address —
For i have known last air — The days grow short — Isn't
time is there left? — Waiting game and we drown —
naked — short — indications enough — at dawn last film
flakes — written on the door the sick lies now are ended
— Vast Thing Police speak into air — any case silence to
answer — i fold in story — A street boy's courage exploded the word — last round into air — like good bye
then — story of absent dreamer — Last September fades
streaked with violence — surges of silence ebbing,
stranded, and we haven't got courage to let go — a great
leisure when you reach September — Days grow short —
Vacant dawn whispers: Game, Hamburger Mary — Five
times terminal — Man, like dawn and dream — Silence to
say 'ebbing carbon dioxide' " —

Outside East St. Louis our revels now are ended —
These events are melted into air — paper forgotten — Yes
you have his bitter spirits — A God bending your summons, commands these visions —

"Like good bye, Johnny — naked, empty as ding-dong
bell — What is St. Louis after *adiós*? — faded story of
absent world just as silver film took it — Remember i was
the movies — Rinse my name for i have known intervention — Pass without doing our ticket — Forgotten
shadow actors walk beside you — mountain wind of Saturn
in the morning sky — From the death trauma weary good
bye then" —

"Intervention overtakes Mr Bradly Mr Martin — distant
coffin in empty room — tape ebbing, picture splintered on
empty flesh — last round, boy — good bye in lips fading
— Remember i was the ship gives no flesh identity" —

"You can say could give no last good bye — In fading breath you can say last round over — stranded, ebbing carbon dioxide, man like identity fading out — Any case a God questions board room circumstances — Remember i was your account — nova dream falling — played the flute in wind and rain streaked with violence — played the Doctor on stage — five times good bye" —

"Last parasite — no shelter — Last morning washed good bye then — stream of distant fingers fading — vaudeville voices absent today — Man questions the dreamer — fade-out overtakes lies — nothing here now but bleeding dream without a shadow without relics — i fold in story of last penny arcade — roller skates before stranded to give you? — hands down — a great leisure in solitude of Saturn" —

Time to squeeze out the welchers, kid, who can't cover their bets and never intended to cover — The "Hassan i Sabbahs" from Cuntville USA backed by yellow assassins who couldn't strangle a hernia — Self-appointed controllers of "the Rotting Kingdom" strictly from Grade B Hollywood who couldn't get their dead nitrous film foot in the door — And all the "Mr Martins" who are trying to buy something for nothing — You can't even con you can't even hustle — You couldn't roll a paralyzed flop — All right all of you cover your bets or shut up and get out of the game — You can take your welching two-bit business to Walgreen's we don't want it — Out out out the whole miserable fucking lot of you — strickly from Moochville —

call the
old doctor
twice ?

You see, son, in this business, welchers who can't cover their bets angle in the "Hassan i Sabbah" from Cuntville strictly from con cop — It's an old vaudeville act — Dead nitrous film foot takes both parts — "Mr Martin," trying to buy a nice quiet easy pitch, you can't even con you can't even hustle — old Western flop — All right all of you cover for a buy or check out — We are walking into the game — Out — Out — A long ride for the white sucking lot of you strictly from heavy metal — Time to squeeze out the dummies — They never intended to cover — But boy the pipes are calling, Cuntville USA — be in the bread line — Self-appointed controllers holding wrist and ankle for a ticket — grade B Hollywood, ghost writing in the sky *The door* — And all the "Mr Martins" won't do you a bit of good on the trip that you're gonna take — something for nothing? — You had every weapon in three galaxies you couldn't roll a paralyzed flop — From Florida up to the old North Pole cover your bets or take your welching two-bit business to Walgreen's — You got the Big Fix down in the hole — Hello yes good bye, Mooch-ville —

Now some write home to orgasm death — welchers, kid, who can't cover their bets — And that "White smoke" — ? ? Man, the "Hassan i Sabbahs" from Cuntville Valley say you are going on a slow boat to China strictly from a big bank roll and a nitrous film foot — if they lost his old blue hands — "Martins" who are trying to buy trips — Can't even con can't even hustle — Quiet — Yes they lost that old flop — All right all of you: *Cover* — So the louder they scream: *Out of the game* — You can take your old ace in the hole to Walgreen's — We don't want it — Strictly from money that they've lost and spent and they may flash a big word line — But as word dust falls they'll be in the bread line without clothes or a dime — "Marks? What marks?" i'm aleaving Martin — Trying to buy that camera gun? It won't do you a bit of good — You can't even con you can't even hustle the trip that I'm gonna take — I've had every con in three galaxies pulled on me — All right, cover that old North Pole or get out of the game — You can take your Big Fix to Walgreen's — Out — Out — Out in the bread line without clothes or a dime the whole sucking lot of you strictly from: *Adiós* —

In three-dimensional terms the board is a group representing international big money who intend to take over and monopolize space — They have their own space arrangements privately owned and consider the governmental space programs a joke — The board books are records pertaining to anyone who can be of use to their program or anyone who could endanger it — The board books are written in symbols referring to association blocks — Like this: $ — "American upper middle-class upbringing with maximum sexual frustration and humiliations imposed by Middle-Western matriarchs" % — "Criminal street boy upbringing — oriented toward money and power — easily corrupted" and so forth — The board agents learn to think in these association blocks and board instructions are conveyed in the board book symbols —

The board is a three-dimensional and essentially stupid pressure group relying on money, equipment, information, files, and the technical brains they have bought — As word dust falls and their control machine is disconnected by partisan activity they'll be in the bread line without clothes or a dime to buy off their "dogs" their "gooks" their "errand boys" their "human animals" — liars — cowards — collaborators — traitors — liars who want time for more lies — cowards who cannot face your "human animals" with the truth — collaborators with insect people, with vegetable people — with any people anywhere who offer them a body forever — traitors to all souls everywhere sold out to shit forever —

"So pack your ermines, Mary — we are getting out of here — i've seen this happen before — Three thousand years in show business — The public is gonna take the place apart" —

"i tell you, boss, the marks are out there pawing the ground — What's this 'Sky Switch'? — What's this 'Reality Con'? What's this 'Tone Scale'? ? — They'll take the place apart — Any minute now — I've seen it happen before on Mercury where we put out a Cool Issue — And the law is moving in fast — Nova Heat — Not locals, boss — This is *Nova Heat* — Well boss?" —

"Call in the Old Doctor" —

Yes when the going gets really rough they call in the Old Doctor to quiet the marks — And he just raises his old blue hands and brings them down slow touching all the marks right where they live and the marks are quiet — But remember, ladies and gentlemen, you can only call the Old Doctor once — So be sure when you call him this is really it — Because if you call the Old Doctor twice he quiets you —

"Here's the Doc now" —

"He's loaded — Throw him under a cold shower — Give him an ammonia coke — Oh my God, they are out there pawing the ground: 'What's this green deal? — What's this mortality con? — You trying to push me down the tone scale, baby? — You trying to short-time some-one, Jack? — Take that heavy metal business to Walgreen's — We don't want it — What's this orgasm death? — Who cooked up these ovens? — What's this white smoke? — Boys, we been subliminated' — How does he look?" —

"Boss, he don't look good — That sneaky pete caught up with him" —

"Oh my God send out Green Tony" —

"Green Tony took off for Galaxy X — On the last saucer, boss — He's coming round now" —

"For God's sake shove him out there with a wing and a prayer" —

The Old Doctor reeled out onto the platform — Then he heard the screaming marks and he steadied himself and he drew all of it into him and he stood up very straight and calm and grey as a wise old rat and he lifted his old blue hands shiny over the dirt and he brought them down slow in the setting sun feeling all the marks so nasty and they just stood there quiet his cold old hands on their wrists and ankles, hands cold and blue as liquid air on wrist and ankle just frozen there in a heavy blue mist of vaporized bank notes —

If you get out there in front of the marks and panic and try to answer them — Well — We don't talk about that

— You see the Old Doctor just draws all that charge and hate right in and uses it all — So the louder they scream and the harder they push the stronger and cooler the Old Doctor is — Yes, son, that's when you know you've got them cooled right — When you can take it all in so the louder they scream and the harder they push the stronger and cooler you are — And then they are quiet — They got nothing more to say and nothing to say it with — You've taken it all all all you got it? (Good, save it for the next pitch) — So there they stand like dummies (they are dummies) and you let your heavy cold blue hands fall down through them — Klunk — cold mineral silence as word dust falls from demagnetized patterns — and your spirals holding wrist and ankle — Where we came in —

Now some wise characters think they can call the Old Doctor twice —

"All right, Doc, get out there and quiet the marks" —

"Marks? What marks? i don't see anybody here but you — All right drop that camera gun — It won't do you a bit of good — i've had every weapon in the galaxy pulled on me" —

"But i got the fix in — i got the Big Fix in" —

"Mister, i am the Big Fix — Hello yes good bye — a few more calls to make tonight" —

You see, son, in this business you always have to find an angle or you'll be in the bread line without clothes or a dime like the song says the angle on planet earth was birth and death — pain and pleasure — the tough cop and the con cop — It's an old vaudeville act — Izzie the Split used to take both parts — But that was in another galaxy — Well it looked like a nice quiet easy pitch — Too quiet like they say in the old Westerns — Fact is we were being set up for a buy and all the money we took was marked — So why did we walk into it? — Fact is we were all junkies and thin after a long ride on the White Subway — flesh junkies, control junkies, heavy metal junkies — That's how you get caught, son — If you have to have it well you've had it — just like any mark — So slide in cool and casual on the next pitch and don't get hooked on the local line: If there is one thing to write on any life form you can score for it's this: Keep your bag packed at all times and ready to travel on —

So pack your ermines, Mary — Write back to the old folks at home — you see this happen before — three thousand years of that old ace in the hole — There was something had to happen and it happened somehow — The Public is gonna take the place apart — He went away but i'm here still — To quiet the marks — He just said "i'm tired of you and i'm checking out" — And they may flash the marks quiet — But boy the pipes the pipes are calling — When you call Him just to raise the price of a ticket — Call the Doc twice? — He quiets you — Here's the Doc now — That old ace in the hole? Good bye old paint i'm aleaving Cheyenne — Ghost writing in the sky trip that you're gonna take — This "Green Deal"? — What's this from Florida up to the old North Pole? — Push me down the tone scale baby, down in the hole? ? In the bread line, Jack — Pick up that heavy metal — *Adiós* — Don't want it —

Now some write home to orgasm death — Who cooked up your dreams? And that "White Smoke"? — Man, we been subliminated — From this valley they say you are going — That sneaky peat bog caught up with him — on a slow boat to China — Green Tony on the last saucer, boss — a big bank roll — a wing and a prayer — without clothes or a dime if they lost his old blue hands over the sky — They'll tell you of trips — in the setting sun — ghost riders in the sky — just stood there quiet — Yes they lost that old hand cold and blue as liquid air — So the louder they scream the old folks at home you'll see me cooler — old ace in the hole — this to say and nothing to say it — He went away —

Money that they've lost and spent like dummies — And they may flash a big word line — But, boy, the pipes the pipes are calling as word dust falls — They'll be in the bread line — holding wrist and ankle just to raise the price of a ticket — now some wise characters — "Marks? What marks? — i'm aleaving ghost writing in the sky — Drop that camera gun — It won't do you a bit of good on the trip that you're gonna take — i've had every weapon in three galaxies pulled on me one time or another — from Florida up to the old North Pole" —

"But i got the Big Fix in — i got the Big Fix down in the hole" —

"In the bread line without clothes or a dime — Hello yes good bye — *Adiós*" —

Well these are the simple facts of the case and i guess i ought to know — There were at least two parasites one sexual the other cerebral working together the way parasites will — That is the cerebral parasite kept you from wising up to the sexual parasite — Why has no one ever asked the question: "What is sex?" — Or made any precise scientific investigation of sexual phenomena? — The cerebral parasite prevented this — And why has no one ever asked: "What is word?" — Why do you talk to yourself all the time? — Are you talking to yourself? — Isn't there someone or something else there when you talk? Put your sex images on a film screen talking to you while you jack-off — Just about the same as the so-called "real thing" isn't it? — Why hasn't it been tried? — And what is word and to whom is it addressed? —Word evokes image does it not? — Try it — Put an image track on screen and accompany it with any sound track — Now play the sound track back alone and watch the image track fill in — So? What is word? — Maya — Maya — Illusion — Rub out the word and the image track goes with it — Can you have an image without color? — Ask yourself these questions and take the necessary steps to find the answers: "What is sex? What is word? What is color?" — Color is trapped in word — Image is trapped in word — Do you need words? — Try some other method of communication, like color flashes — a Morse code of color flashes — or odors or music or tactile sensations — Anything can represent words and letters and association blocks — Go on try it and see what happens — science pure science — And what is love? — Who do you love? — If i had a talking picture of you would i need you? Try it — Like i say put your sex image on screen talking all the sex words — Hide simple facts of the case: two parasites one sexual, the other electric voice of C — Well the board as you listen fills in — I ought to know —Cerebral parasite kept you from wising up board books written in symbols of sexual parasite — Pressure group relying on rectum while you jack-off — Control "real thing" — collaborators with image trapped in word — What is word? Word is an array of calculating machines — Spots of weakness opened up by the track goes with it — The Ovens smell of simple facts of the case and i guess won't be much left — little time, parasites — Now we see all the pictures — Cerebral phonograph talks sex scenes — And this pubescent word evokes images does it not? Look and accompany it with human nights and watch the image track fill in — Stranger lips bring down the word forever — Word falling — Photo falling — hide nor hair — at the club insane orders and counterorders — stranger on the shore — My terminal electric voice of C, where's it going to get me? — Lover, please forget about the tourists — i said the Chief of Police after hours — This thing D.C. called love — You better move on — British Prime Minister, say it again — Hear you, Switzerland — Freeze all living is easy — My heart to mindless idiot — It had to be you — You won't cut word lines? — Found the somebody who — It's electric storms of violence — Any advantage precariously held — June July and August walk on — Pinball-led streets — i'm going home, drugstore woman — Show you something: berserk machine — One more time, Johnny Angel? — with short time secondhand love? — nothing but The Reality Concession to set up a past — Workers paid off in thing called "Love" — the junk man at the outskirts —

Gongs of violence and how show stranger on the shore — Real Mr Bradly Mr Martin charges in — "Where's it going to get me? — Artists take over" — counterorders and the living is easy — it's orbit of the Saturn Galaxy — Snap your fingers — dreams end everything — hide nor

hair — at the club actually be your way — Time — It's
stranger on the shore — After hours this secondhand
trade-in called "Love" — You better move on — Tentative
flesh — So good night — Say it again — Face sucked into
other apparatus — now trading mornings — So pack your
ermines, Mary — You see this happen before — Stranger
on the shore my real ace in the hole — June July August
walk on — The public is going to take the place — I'm
going home — Nothing but Green Tony on the last
saucer, boss —

Word falling, photo falling, old folks at home — You'll
see me guess orders and counterorders — And they flash
a big word pay-off — But boy the pipes the pipes are
calling as you listen — Big money be in the bread line —
wising up — scandinavia outhouse parasite just to raise
the price of a ticket — Word flesh group relying on rectum
— Now we see all the pictures feeling along — And this
pubescent word covered orgasm death on a slow boat
to China — Stranger lips bring roll call — Rectum suddenly released as he melted nitrous film flesh — Word is
an array of calculating machines from Florida up to the
old North Pole — Image track goes with it — Ovens down
in the hole — Won't be much left — In the bread line —
Adiós — Now we see all the pictures —

Enter George Raft groom *cum* chauffeur — He lurked
hat and collar and hands in his pockets — Heavy with
menace he takes the job of looking after someone who was
sure to reach the film — Sticky end abroad — George Raft
went home talking — Smoothest of all the tough guys
tiring from films altogether — a little fleshier around the
jaw suite but available for civilian jobs — Those eyes still

snap and this ain't Hamlet — I want hunched tight hipped
purpose — Action — Camera — Take — Hanging stays as
butler — 500 full-time officials — The death penalty will
not be scrapped as transport, Mr Workers' Union — You'll
find it waiting down shadow pools — The try begins with
BOAC — sufficient spurts that traditionally service transient hotels with rose wallpaper — Attempt is now in
Rome with the film — red nitrous fumes over you —
Young witness circumstances brown ankles — Naked for
physical factory rushed to execution marriage — Two
boys mutually stylized hover the vigil till execution image
back to hotel room in London — Harm begins in Britain
from his face — cobblestone lane pageant — shirt flapping pants slide down — felt execution marriage —
Stanley Spencer left that mess — Who is that naked
corpse? — Sex would die on the answer — Around in
biographer languorously sure that there is me-you cock
flipped out and up as one is or need be a boy in kerosene
lamp light — old dead-pan anecdotal sage for transient
hotels — "Bend over you" — young conceived in this
cook book — Pants down to the ankle his first sexual
experience convinced him that carnal love reproduces
feedback from vacant lot — laughing suburb boys quiet
elegant and soft stay in close — His style is cool like his
head was sewed on a Russian version of James Dean —
filtering black aphrodisiac ointment in Spanish fly that
will take photo turnstile through flesh — Two faces tried
to rush entirely into his face — He was in the you-me in
you with all the consequences — burning outskirts of the
world — Character took my hands in dash taught you

from last airport typical of his decision to intersect on new kind of daring in memory of each other —

"I say nothing and nothing is now in Rome with the film — Intersected eleventh hour paper — Star failed yesterday — Screen went dead — Young face melted" —

"Good bye then — I thought entirely into the room with me — Panama" —

From San Diego up to Maine Solemn Accountants are jumping ship forever —

"Word falling, photo falling, sir — In the last skimpy surplus, sir, orders and counterorders — Stranger outside, sir" they said — "And what's it going to get me?" —

Allies wait on knives — Street gangs had to be you — You won't cut word lines? — From a headline of penniless migrants electric storms of violence — Our show and we're proud of August walk-on — Her Fourth-Grade Class screamed in terror — Pinball-led Street of the Dogs — I looked at the pavement — Show you something: berserk machine — Pavement was safer — stale streets of yesterday? — short time secondhand love? Workers paid off in thing conditions? —

Delusion of death going — Artists take over — Was it easy? — Only this should have been obvious: orbit Of the Saturn Galaxy — Only live animals write anything — hide nor hair at the club — after hours this liz replica synthesized from tentative flesh — So pack your ermines, Mary, you of later and lesser crimes pudgy and not pretty —

"Will Hollywood never learn?" —

"On the last saucer, boss" —

Unimaginable disaster — You'll see me guess time — It

is impossible to estimate the damage — And they may flash streams in the area, but boy the pipes the pipes are calling — in Ewyork, Onolulu, Aris, Ome, Oston that old ace in the hole — past crimes feeling along your time —

Enter George Raft *cum* Paris in the Spring all his hands in his pockets — Heavy with the Japanese Sandman — Looking for someone who was trading new dreams for old —

"Unchain my broad" —

George Raft went home tiring from films altogether — but available for civilian jobs — once in a while — sticky end for Old Black Bird — "Martin's reality film is the dreariest entertainment ever presented to a captive audience." He stated flatly. The opening scene shows a man sitting in the bar of a luxury hotel clearly he has come a long way travel-stained and even the stains unfamiliar cuff links of a dull metal that seem to absorb light . . the room buzzes with intrigue . . Mauritania . . Uranium . . Oil . . War . . This man and what he sees are *in the film* . . Clearly portentous exciting events are about to transpire. Now take the same man *outside the film* . . He has come a long way and the stains are all too familiar . . An American tourist confides in the bartender:

"Now Mother is down with a bad case of hemorrhoids and we don't speak the language I tried to tell this doctor at least he called himself a doctor and I want your advice about the car . . Oh here's the man who took us to the Kasbah? How much shall I give him?" . . He pulls a wad of bills from his pocket raw eager thrust of an overtip the magic gesture that makes a man bow three times and disappear into a dollar . . A gnat has fallen into the man's sherry. Clearly no portentous exciting events are about to transpire. You will readily understand why people will go to any lengths to get in the film to cover themselves with any old film scrap . . junky . . narcotics agent . . thief . . informer . . anything to avoid the hopeless dead-end horror of being just who and where you all are: dying animals on a doomed planet.

Martin's film worked for a long time. Used to be most everybody had a part in the film and you can still find remote areas where a whole tribe or village is on set. Nice to see but it won't do you much good. Even as late as the 1920's everybody had a good chance to get in the film.

Well he was dipping into the till. Just looks at me and says "Account sheets are empty many years." The film stock issued now isn't worth the celluloid its printed on. There is nothing to back it up. The film bank is empty. To conceal the bankruptcy of the reality studio it is essential that no one should be in position to set up another reality set. The reality film has now become an instrument and weapon of monopoly. The full weight of the film is directed against anyone who calls the film in question with particular attention to writers and artists. Work for the reality studio or else. Or else you will find out how it feels to be *outside the film*. I mean literally without film left to get yourself from here to the corner . ." Every object raw and hideous sharp edges that tear the uncovered flesh.

Who's sorry now? — I say nothing and nothing is now in Rome with the film — Intersected eleventh hour paper — Young witness or old hear the Japanese Sandman —

shuffle
cut

"Pack your ermines, Mary" — (Female impersonators pack in shabby dressing room — riot noises in the distance — Scene opens into other dressing rooms and transient hotels — switch to office of the Carny Manager — riot noises moving closer — police whistles, machine guns, slamming shop shutters — cut-ups of riot newsreels) —

"What's this reality con?" — (Vista of tombstones and lavatories — hospitals, flophouses, asylums — grey dishwater smell of institution cooking — whine of dying people — "Lord, Lord, i don't even feel like a human" — "So we drove down to St. Petersburg and Mother didn't like it at all" — The riot noises swell to a vast adolescent muttering — boys armed with switchblades and bicycle chains — A cobblestone shatters the window of the carny office — As the outside air rushes in the carny manager coughs and sputters — "And the law is moving in fast" — (Nova police stand before a switchboard that lights up as their agents make arrest and question suspects — "I'm not taking the rap for those board bastards — i'm going to rat on everybody" — The lights extend, closing round the board —

"The marks are out there pawing the ground" — (riot shots of all times and places) —

"What's this Green Deal?" — (Green vegetable junkies suck oxygen of the earth) —

"You trying to short-time someone, Jack?" — (subliminal

slow motion on the screen — venereal disease films at 35 frames per second) —

"Take that heavy metal business to Walgreen's" — (heavy metal junkies on the nod in a blue mist of vaporized bank notes)—

"What's this orgasm death?" — (Ejaculating bodies hang from gallows goosed by giggling green street boys — Condemned prisoners twist in cyanide fumes under civil leer of the witness — Middle-aged cardiac dies on the young model who pushes the corpse away in disgust — "Horrible old character got physical and died in me") —

"Who cooked up these ovens?" — flash prisoners in the ovens — lattice of white-hot metal closing round them — phosphorescent smoldering shag heaps of Minraud —

heat cutting off the sources of animal life — Crabs sidle from cone-shaped nests — "Zero eaten by crab") —

"What's this 'White Smoke' "? — (Sick addicts in precinct cells give off the colorless no-smell of death — A white smoke spreads over the blighted earth) —

"Boys we been subliminated" — (Newspapers, magazines, muttering voices on TV and radio — "birth and death and the human condition — always been that way and always will — Besides you can't do anything — Don't stick your neck out — Don't get ulcers") —

"Call in the Old Doctor" — (The doctor on stage — He sucks all the newsreels of riot and hate faces into him — Riot pictures freeze to stills as he brings his hands down — Klunk) —

"Now some wise characters think they can call the Old Doctor twice" — (Newsreels and riot noises shut off — Cold blue silence of interstellar space closes round the board table — A guard reaches for his vibrating camera gun — "Won't do you a bit of good — had every weapon in the galaxy pulled on me one time or another" — Flash Ovens — Flash Orgasm Sting — White Smoke drifts away and leaves the doctor still standing there — board books spread out on the table like a pack of tarot cards — The doctor folds the cards together — The board disappears in a silver flash) — "He quiets you" —

And so we turn over the board books written in symbols of a time that meanwhile i had forgotten — Like this: $ — American scent of memory pictures — sexual frustration — Scandinavia outhouse skin put it on — % — criminal street boy of dying peoples — easily corrupted and shoved humiliations — Away from me, these association locks — Pictures shatter a window in stupid pressure group relying on rectum — Board members, look out — Technical brains melted the law — Control machine is disconnected by nova police — Look at the bread line — Their boy entered the '20s in drag from collaborators — Liars spread slow-motion flashes — Board book symbols refer to association locks — information files of human nights there — collaborators with any people anywhere on dead nitrous flesh — Traitors to all souls everywhere travel there — As word dust falls cross newsprint of the earth, voices won't do a bit of good — The Old Doctor cleaving a heavy frustration and humiliation account — Hurry up please — The board is near right now relying on money, fading voices — Control machine is disconnected — Word fell out of here through the glass and metal streets — God of Panic pipes blue notes through dying peoples — The law is dust — The wired structure of reality went up in slow-motion flashes —

Invisible intervention of a time forgotten — slow water dripping on a garage — voices in other dressing rooms — "Turn around — Bend over" — poisonous cloud of other flesh — Scandinavia outhouse skin on the co-pilot — Sat helpless while the invading force guided humiliations —

"You see, son, we were the only riders — Mutual erections fading through dusty air of gymnasiums — Folding cocks disappear on dead nitrous flesh — Point of these exercises is to maintain the local line — Sinking ship trying source of frustration to buy ersatz summons" —

Yes, you have a doorway — Ali blew the smoke and waved his hands — "Abracadabra" — distant events in green neon — you the smoke — The man laughed — Ali, muttering in the dog rotation — old mirror bent over a chair — controlled drum music on the crumpled form — Many names murmur cloth that fell in a heap — Flute went out shutting the door — luminous grey flakes falling — Galaxies pulled green troops in the streets — Impressions suddenly collapse to a heap — (Motions with his hand) — Guards fold now — Dodging from side to side over spots of weakness opened a great rent — Now Ali doubled back from above punch cards — There was nothing but a smear of grey substance barring his way to the towers — Film set goes up in red nitrous smoke — Remember show price? Know who I am? Yes talking to you board members . . I don't talk often and I don't talk long . . You smell Hiroshima? You know who I am now? *Señor* Deadline has come to call . . Did you think you could call me and not pay you welching board bastards?

Set your Geiger counters forward an hour. Captain Clark welcomes you aboard . . last rights . . Mr Deadline is *here* to call . .

(The concept of Deadliners I owe to a story that appeared in *New World Science Fiction* . . Nova Publications . . 7 Grape St. High Holborn London Vol 49 June . . "The Star Virus" by J. Barryington Bayley . . Deadliners in this story are space travelers across light-years who have lost all human contacts and fears. They play a form of nuclear poker. Calling in this game can explode the players and the premises . .)

"Why you might have taken half the planet with you," exclaims an inexperienced Deadliner . .

"The whole of it, mate."

"You touched a pack of cards — You see, son, voices muttering in the dog rotation: 'Pain and pleasure — orgasm death — flesh' — desolate underbrush of old Westerns — battered phonograph sex scenes — courage to pass without doing things — If you'll just stay near right now — be shifted harsh at the Ovens — Mutual erections fading, kid — Have to square it with him — We were all junkies and dead train whistles the local line — Look down along a brass bed — Many names murmur of human nights there — i am dying cross newspapers of the earth — Stranger lips bring down death — breathless flute through Ali's body — fading my name — newsreels of riot frozen to stills — whiffs of evening breeze" —

"Call the Old Doctor twice? — cleaving a summons — Marks closed your account — Hurry up, please — There is only the silence of water smiles dimmer at the edges — I don't see anybody here — You made a wide U turn back to camera gun — Vaudeville voices won't do you a bit of good — green troops in the area — The White Smoke drifts away" —

"But i got the area trade — Impressions of Present Time" —

Makes a folding motion with his hands — Guards fold together and disappear — People gone — Well fade out in other flesh armed with switchblades and bicycle chains — Pictures shatter a window in the office — Spattered light on naked rectum — Young faces melted the law in dead nitrous streets — Errand boys closing round the board —

"What's this green boy entered the '20s in drag from sinking ship?" —

"You trying sources of slow-motion flashes on the screen?" —

"Boneless mummy was death in the last Walgreen's — We don't want it" —

"We been subliminated in doorway" —

Errand boy from last parasite muttering beside you — great wind voices on those tracks — remitted muttering: "Not think the Doctor on stage" and "Who am i to say more?" —

Empty all the hate faces sucked into fear — crumpled cloth bodies — open shirt flapping — some wise characters — All right, doctor — Vapor trails writing the sky — Newsreels shut off — Magazines screaming on the parasite — The radio muttering — "The Doctor on stage" —

All the hate faces sucked into release without more ado what? — bodies and water everywhere — The Oven rousers gave off a stench of rotten lips departed — Move in fast — Interrogate substance of the other — Boneless mummy moved with the speed of "want it?" Empty flesh of KY and rectal mucus last gate from human form — They twisted through open shirt flapping against each other — Hands goosed the ass — Penis spurted again — the gate from burning sex skin — Empty faces sucked in other apparatus —

great wind voices beside you — the Doctor on stage — "Out of here, female impersonators" — orgasm of memory pictures — people gone —

"All right, doctor, before newsreels shut off indications enough — i told you i would come back beside him — He could move now — healed scars — courage to pass without doing pictures" —

"i'm going now — We were all junkies — Now some wise characters think guards and weapons of the enemy were all right — Suddenly shut off with camera gun and static — We see all the Garden of Delights in a flash like a pack of cards — He felt a little pleasure — sex scenes of all times" —

"Old Doctor twice? Cleaving a heavy erogenous message reflected in your account —Hurry up, please — empty flesh dimmer at the edges — God of Panic piping blue notes touched a pack of cards — Through the glass we see all the pictures — invisible orgasm death skin on the co-pilot — Battered phonograph talks humiliations — Poisonous cloud near right now" —

"Fading, kid — Voices in other dressing with the St. Louis suburb — The local line bends over rectum of broken nights — Fading my name through dying air" —

in
that game?

The Fluoroscopic Kid says: "Now look, son, when you move in on a new pitch don't be one of these Eager Beavers jump right into a dime — That's how you got caught here in the Cycle of Action — Now learn to sit back and watch — Don't talk don't play just *watch* — fifty a hundred thousand years if necessary until you know all the rules and combos penalties and angles — When you can see all the cards then move in and take it all — Learn to *watch* and you *will* see all the cards — Look through the human body the house passes out at the door — What do you see? — It is composed of thin transparent sheets on which is written the action from birth to death — Written on "the soft typewriter" *before* birth — a cold deck built in — The house know every card you will be dealt and how you will play all your cards — And if some wise guy does get a glimmer and maybe plays an unwritten card:

"Green Tony — Izzy the Push — Sammy the Butcher — *Hey Rube!!!* Show this character the Ovens — This is a wise guy" —

You want to sit in on that game? ? — Now look some more — The body is two halves stuck together like a mold — That is, it consists of *two* organisms — See "the Other Half" invisible — (to eyes that haven't learned to watch) — Like a Siamese twin ten thousand years in show business engaged by a silver cord to all erogenous zones — lives along the divide line — is an amphibious two-sexed actor half-man half-woman — double-gated either sex can breathe air or the underwater medium up your mother's snatch — "the Other Half" is "You" next time around — born when you die — that is when "the Other Half" kills you and takes over — (Take a talking picture of you. Now stop the projector and sound track frame by frame: stop . . go go go . . stop . . go go . . *Stop*. When the sound track stops it stops.When the projector stops a still picture is on screen. This would be your last picture the last thing you saw. Your sound track consists of your body sounds and sub-vocal speech. Sub-vocal speech *is* the word organism the "Other Half." spliced in with your body sounds. You are convinced by association that your body sounds will stop if sub-vocal speech stops and so it happens. Death is the final separation of the sound and image tracks. However, once you have broken the chains of association linking sub-vocal speech with body sounds shutting off sub-vocal speech need not entail shutting off body sounds and consequent physical death.)

Now let's play some poker — Why not take over both halves of a body so you don't need any mooching "Other Half" — Why not rewrite the message on "the soft type-writer"? — Why not take the board books and rewrite all message? — Why not take over the human body right down the middle line? — Under distant fingers move in and take it all — All right, watch what is covering the two halves with so-called human body — Flesh sheets on which is written: "The spines rubbed and merged" — Written *before* on "the Soft Typewriter" — transparent quivering substance the body is two halves stuck together around him — a shadowy figure melting to sperm — a silver cord of tendril fingers rubbing erogenous zones along the divide line — contractions in the tumescent sponge pulse future organism — shoot out body dies falling into water — Play some poker — Why not take over underwater sleep? — You don't need any "Other Half" — Why not take the middle line? You see it is composed from birth to death — A cold deck under his gills dealt the softening spine — In that game? — Now look again — He sank into other flesh mold — Siamese twin substance in spine lives along the shocks of electric cocaine pleasure — The Other Half will be born inside feeling both halves of the body —

Now *look* son, when you move in a new angle — These Eager Beavers jump right into a dime — That way Birth & Death cycle action — You want out? Con cop — It's an old vaudeville act — Just walk in and throw the tin on the board —

Learn to sit back and watch — Just take both parts — Watch what you walk into — So called human body? Long ride on the White Sheets — Slide in cool and casual — I'll play your cards — You want to sit in on the local line? — Look down look down along that line before you travel there — If there the body is two halves stuck together form you can score for —

Why I'm here — To play some poker — Why not flash the marks soft typewriter? Why not call? — When you call write all message — Why not take over ticket? You want out? — Con cop — It's an old vaudeville act — Just walk in and throw the tin on the Board — Cover Sammy and the boys — Take the board books and rewrite the cold deck — Any board member want to play some straight five card stud? I didn't think so — Now cut up the board books, son — Minutes to go —

The Subliminal Kid is a charter defector from the nova mob —

"Just a technical sergeant is all — Just Time — Just Time — Just Time — " So he moved in with the Rewrite Department and set up his headquarters to put out the Rewrite Bulletins on subliminal level — It's all done with tape recorders. Go out and buy three fine machines on credit and put your name down for an in-television unit. Find a boy with blue eyes and gentle precise fingers . . (He was a ham radio operator at twelve at the age of eight he released weather balloons which he fabricated from plastic suit covers . .) The boy will wire your machines for you. You need a switchboard so you can control the machines: Tape Recorder 1 playback five seconds Tape Recorder 2 and 3 record and so forth. Take an everyday situation you are arguing with your boy friend or girl friend remembering what was said last time and thinking of things to say next time the whole stupid argument going going round and round like the music in your head until it bores you just silly to hear it but you are aggrieved and playing back self-pity and you just can't shut up. Take your arguments and complaints and put them on T.R.1 and call that machine Tom or Dick or Harry you name it it's yours. On T.R.2 put all the things he or she said to you or might say. Now make the two machines talk: T.R.1 playback five seconds T.R.2 record. T.R.2 playback three seconds T.R.1 record. Run it through fifteen minutes half an hour now switch intervals. Run the interval switch you used on T.R.1 back on T.R.2. — (You will find that the intervals are as important as the so-called context) — listen to the two machines mixing it around and around. Now for T.R.3 — (Who is the third that walks beside you?) — With T.R.3 you can introduce the factor of "irrelevant response" so put just any old thing on T.R.3 a sad old tune a sad old joke a piece of the street TV radio and cut T.R.3 into the argument T.R.1: "I waited up for you last night till two o'clock" . . T.R.3: "And now if you will excuse me . . The soccer scores are coming in from the capitol . . One must pretend an interest . ."

Get it out of your head and into the machines. Stop talking stop arguing. Let the machines talk and argue. A tape recorder is an externalized section of the human nervous system. You can find out more about the nervous system and gain more control over your reaction by using a tape recorder than you could find out sitting twenty years in the lotus posture. Whatever your problem is just throw it into the machines and let them chew it around a while. There is of course the initial problem: programming tape recorders is an expensive deal any way you wire it.

The spliced-tape experiment to which I have already referred can be performed by anyone equipped with two tape recorders connected by extension lead so he can record directly from one machine to the other. Since the experiment may give rise to a marked erotic reaction it is more interesting to select as your partner for this experiment some one with whom you are on intimate terms. We have two subjects designated as S and W. Now take a text any text. S records the text on Tape Recorder 1. W records the same text on Tape Recorder 2. Now play back T.R.1 three seconds recording on T.R.2. Play back T.R.2

three seconds recording on T.R.1 and so forth *alternating* the two recorded voices. This is the simplest form of the spliced-tape experiment. The same results can be obtained by splicing two street recordings made separately by S and W. In order to obtain any degree of precision the tapes must be cut with a scissors and spliced together with tape. This is a laborious process that can be appreciably expedited if you have access to a cutting room and use film tape which is larger and much easier to handle. You can carry the experiment further by taking a talking film of S and a talking film of W and splicing sound and image track alternating 24 times per second.

S and W carry in their respective and presumed separate nervous systems the equipment to record and playback sound to take images, equipment of which recorder and camera are the externalized abstraction. The equipment contained in the nervous systems of our two subjects is capable of *total recording* that is of recording and storing sound image smell tactile sensations and the affective reactions associated with this material. The total recording is activated by the playback of sound and image track by precise association with it, so that when we cut the film and sound record made on recorder and camera by our two subjects in together we are splicing the total record of S in with the total record of W. A flu virus is able to take over a healthy lung cell by giving the same signals as a healthy lung cell. The virus can give the same signals as a healthy lung cell because *it was a healthy lung cell at one time.* Spliced tape and film may or may not give rise to virus forms — (*Warning: experiments with spliced tape and film are dangerous* parenthetically) — In any

case a unit of sound track recorded and film taken by S
spliced in with W is now able to give the same signals as a
W unit because it *was that unit by the fact of being recorded on W's sound and image track* and replacing the
sound and image unit recorded and filmed by W. We may
say that S can give the same signals as W *because he
retroactively was* W when an S unit of sound and image is
cut into W's sound and image track replacing W with S.
Of course the same replacements are occurring in the
sound and image track of S. *If S is spliced into the total
record of W and W is not spliced into the total record of
S this unilateral splicing may result in W contracting an S
virus to his considerable disadvantage.*

Many applications of the spliced-tape principle will
suggest themselves to the alert reader. Suppose you are
some creep in a grey flannel suit. You want to present a
new concept of advertising to the Old Man . . *creative advertising:* "I mean advertisements that tell a story and
create characters Inspector J. Lee of the Nova Police
smokes Players — (flashes his dirty rotten hunka tin).
Agent K 9 uses a Bradly laser gun. Aurelius would have
approved your favorite smoke. Advertisements should pro-
vide the same entertainment value as the content of a
magazine. Call in the best writers to write the continuity
the best painters and photographers on the layout. *Your*
product *deserves* the best." So before he goes up against
the Old Man he records the Old Man's voice and splices
his own voice in explaining his new concept and puts it
out on the office air-conditioning system. Or suppose you
are a singer. Well splice your singing in with the Beatles,
the Rolling Stones, the Animals. Splice yourself in with

newscasters, prime ministers, presidents. Why stop there? Why stop anywhere? Everybody splice himself in with everybody else. Communication must be made total. only way to stop it.

Wittgenstein said: "No proposition can contain itself as an argument" = The only thing *not* prerecorded in a prerecorded universe is the prerecording itself which is to say *any* recording that contains a random factor.

It's all done with tape recorders . . Guess you've all seen the Philipp's Carry Corder a handy machine for street recording and playback you can carry it under your coat for recording important thing to remember is not just recording but *playback in the street* the Carry Corder looks like a transistor radio for street playback city folks don't notice yesterday voices phantom car holes in time . . fun and games with this gadget . . God's little toy Paul Bowles calls it . . (Maybe his last toy parenthetically he is gone away through unknown mornings leave a million tape recordings of his voice behind fading into the cold spring air pose a colorless question?) . . Why not give Carry Corder parties? Every guest arrives with his Carry Corder and cartridges of what he intends to say recording what other Carry Corders say to him it is the height of rudeness not to record when directly addressed by another Carry Corder no one can talk *directly* at a Carry Corder party if you want to say something you have to nick off into the little boy's room and record it first while your genial host mixes the whole party around on a battery of tape recorders . . ("Not infrequently I stripped to the waist and pitched in with the men . . Yes boys that's me there by the cement mixer.") . . You can use the re-

cordings from the last party at the next party funeral
meats serving up the wedding feast in the word of the
Immortal Bard tomorrow and tomorrow and tomorrow . .
And think what several hundred people with Carry Corders could do at a political rally . . Carry your Carry
Corders down Fleet St. and Madison Avenue . . Sublimi-
nate the subliminators . . Carry Corders of the world
unite. You have nothing to lose but your prerecordings.

"It's all done with recorders — The sound track evokes
the image track — Recollect when i was on the Madison
Avenue Lark — So i am giving out with a steady stream
of interviews and i soon extracted the interview formulae
— I recorded ten alternative answers to any question from
the interview framework — And all i had to do was press
buttons and out came the answers — I could of course do
this from a distance by radio and retired to my Southern
plantation strictly from Tin Pan Alley with recorded
darkies singing out in the mimosa and Spanish moss projected on view screens — Later the whole operation was
automatic and did not need my attention at all and i had
answers for the next thousand years all set up — I extended the principle of absent control to other activities
— I dictated the necessary orders, counterorders and alternative moves for any operation — I could write all the
speeches and ultimatums of one government with answering speeches and ultimatums of another and of course
put on the war recordings when the order came through
channels — Just a technical sergeant know how things are
done — Same method can be applied to sex — As a young
man i discovered that i could anticipate the dialogue of
any amorous encounter — So i recorded the dialogue and

made an image track to go with it — appropriate background music, lighting, odors the lot — Action — Camera — Compliments of Pavlov i could do quite as well with my recordings as with the so-called "real thing" (The image track can be dispensed with once the appropriate associations are established) — i built up a whorehouse of tapes and rented them out for two notes a night any script any face you want — Spot of bother with the Syndicate and that's when i moved into the Madison Avenue Territory — Now carry it a bit further — The interviewer can of course apply the same method — That is record his questions and alternative questions — Both governments can record speeches, ultimatums, orders and counterorders — So record the whole war with its battles and sieges, victories and defeats, monumental fuck-ups and corny songs — Lovers exchange tapes — You understand nobody has to be there at all — So why ask questions and why answer? — Why give orders and why make speeches? — Why not leave your tape with her tape and dispense with sexual contact? — And then? — Since no one is there to listen, why keep running the tape? — Why not shut the whole machine off and go home? Exactly what i intend to do — Turn all my tapes over to Rewrite and go home — You can look any place — No good — *No bueno* — Departed have left no address — It's all done with tape recorders. What we see is dictated by what we hear. You can verify this by a simple experiment. Turn off the sound track on your television set and use an arbitrary recorded sound track from your tape recorder: street sounds . . music . . conversation. . recordings of other TV programs, radio et cetera.You will find that the arbitrary sound track seems to be appropriate . . people running for a bus in Piccadilly with a sound track of machine-gun fire looks like 1917 Petrograd. You can extend the experiment by using material that is more or less appropriate to the image track. For example take a political speech on TV shut off sound track and substitute another speech you have prerecorded . . hardly tell the difference . . isn't much . . Record the sound track of one Danger Man spy program and substitute for another . . Try it on your friends and see if they can't tell the difference.

The sound track conjures up the image track — Word came before image — Shut off the sound track on your TV set and put in your own sound track words music what you will — Now play back your sound track and you will see the images sharp and clear — I recorded sound tracks of TV and film programs — mixing in suggestions from Rewrite to microphones and radio cruise cars — So i press a button and record all sounds and voices of the city — So i press a button to feed back these sounds with cut-ins a few seconds later, you are still watching a TV program or listening to the juke box — A few seconds later you are hearing the same words from my broadcast with cut-ins from Rewrite — Of course i cut in bulletins from Rewrite with all popular songs using music as punctuation — (Singing came before talking) — I folded the bulletins in with newspapers, magazines and novels — I put them out mixed with street sounds and talk wind and rain and lapping water and birdcalls — Well — Word evokes image — & % $ $ "N:? — Singing came before talking — Shut the whole machine off — Rub out the word — There is no one there to hear it — Nothing here now but the recordings may not refuse vision in setting forth — the story of one absent today — Fade-out overtakes Mr Bradly Mr Martin — Five times thy strong tape caught in the door — no shelter in the dogs of unfamiliar dust — the cold *adiós* without a shadow — These our actors bid you a long good night —

showed you
your air

"The Subliminal Kid charters your attention please — i am Inspector J. Lee of The Nova Police — Just a technical sergeant moved a nova criminal to Rewrite Operations — And i am sure that it's all done with recorders — Remember that these techniques for the next thousand years manipulated by nova criminals — Absent control simple: Always create as many insoluble counterorders and alternative conflicts recordings to the explosion of a planet — Recording devices fix the nature of absolute associations, established total weapons — manipulated on a global scale feeds: Go home — Conflicts are deliberately created — No address the Nova Mob — Sammy the Butcher, the sound track conjures up the Brown Artist to paint yellow plains of Minraud — Jacky Blue Note, shut off the sound track on your Hamburger Mary — the subliminal words music what you will — Now in all my experience as a police officer never seen such total fear of indicated alterations on any planet — The same words straighten out this mess — Cut in bulletins from Rewrite — Nothing here now but unworkable course — Mr Bradly

Mr Martin, Audience Chamber with the threat of no shelter in the dogs — Is that clear enough or shall i make it even clearer?" —

"For i have known exactly what i intend to do" —

"Isn't time is there left? — Go home — A boy shut off the sound track on you in the door — words, music what you will — Now the final ape of history sees the images sharp and clear on your ticket that exploded — end of voices — So i press a button beside you and the dreamer gone — So why ask questions and why intersect on empty speech? — Why not leave this dream contact? Shut the machine off — nothing here now but the door — juke box bulletins from Rewrite singing in newspapers and magazines of the earth:

"Word falling — Photo falling — Defectors from the Nova Mob — Just time — Just time — Just time" —

Electric storms of violence sweep broadcast still in progress "Word falling — Photo falling" —

"Gongs of violence show alternative answers to any question — Artists take over the entire answer battery of automatic junk state — i extended this to other flesh — Counterorders issued — Dictate force of riot police at the operation — Death Dwarfs on orbit of Saturn galaxy — The interviewers shift in speed-up movie — Now since i could attack position over instrument i had the answers for a thousand years — Didn't have to be there answering questions of absent tenants — The Rewrite Doctor on stage — shatters a window in image without word — All i had to do was press slow-motion flashes and newsreels shut off — All right, Doctor, stop asking questions — Indications enough answer without being there — Shut the whole machine off July, 1962, Present Time — Big money bulletins feed back Scandinavia outhouse parasite — A song goes through the city with suggestion pictures feeling along — And this broadcast was still in progress — The human body is an image on screen talking — You made questions and put the answers on a face — Good bye old interview — Mack The Knife, i can work for anybody — Juke box or radio speak of new dreams for old — Moanin' low my sweet bulletins and feed them back all the time to put all the things you are on subliminal level — Alternative answers to any question can play the game as well as you — Entire answer battery on automatic hopes to be there — i could control it from my blue heaven — Somebody stole my girl — Thing was automatic — Seemed to whisper Louise, Mary, all the things you used to do — Should old acquaintance go home? Why should anybody be there from Florida up to the old North Pole? — Ahead — Ahead — Ahead — they chanted and retired to Tin Pan Alley — Record either end — Beat your mother to Spanish moss — automatic future for the next thousand years — war recordings at the time but Old Bill, returned a technical sergeant — Witnesses from a distance observed the image track streak across the sky and crash with associations — established this art along the Tang dynasty — So we turn over board books on subliminal level — sexual frustration lark — 'So i am giving out skin — Put it on' — easily ten alternative answers to any association locks — And all i had to do was shatter a window in stupid board members — Errand boy closing their screens — the whole operation from collaborators and liars — Won't be much left — i dictated the necessary orders on the air — with human nights — Voices came through channels — just any people anywhere on dead nitrous flesh are done — i discovered that i could anticipate the humiliation account" —

"Hurry up — Counter" —

"So i recorded the dialogue and boy from last stupid pressure group with appropriate background music — Control machine is disconnected compliments of Pavlov — board books are written in symbols as the so-called 'real thing' — American from last interview performed sharp discharge from method — So why ask questions and why answers $? — Why not leave your tape humiliations and Scandinavia outhouse contacts? — You can look any place — no pressure group relying on rectum — no address — Technical brains melted the law — The sound track conjures up the image police — Shut off the sound track — Their boy entered the '20s in word and music — Spread slow-motion flashes and you see the image sharp and clear — So i press the button blocks board instructions cross newspapers of the earth — Collaborators with word with flesh, traitors to all souls everywhere, i cut in bulletins from Rewrite with heavy punctuation — The board is relying on fading voices — Shut the whole machine off — Rub out the board — Is near right now to hear it — Mr Bradly Mr Martin five times guided poisonous cloud of parasites — These our actors bid you peaceful opaqueness in this monument of tiredness" — The Old Man himself stood at the end of the board room table a hat box under his arm. With an abrupt movement he emptied the hat box. The bronze head of a young girl crudely severed with a hack saw clattered across the board room table. The Old Man held up a hack saw bronze filings caught in its teeth.

"This old hand went and sawed the head off their filthy mermaid . . J. Ericson & Sisters only living rival of Trak . . . If anyone does not like this thing that I have done I can use this saw a second time."

He paced behind the board members like an aroused tom cat. He stopped behind Scamperelli the Pulp King who perfected a process for making pasta from sawdust. He clamped one hand over Scamperelli's mouth pulled his head back and applied the hack saw to Scamperelli's throbbing carotid. "Scamperelli do you like this thing that I have done?"

"Glub . . glub . . glub . ."

"I presume that is pulp talk for 'yes.' "

He paced and stopped behind the Oil King. "Total Oil, do you like this thing that I have done?"

Dry Hole Dutton glanced sideways at the saw. With a presence of mind derived from his wildcatting days he crooned out: "Only you can make the world go round." Unanimously other board members took up the chant. Its the old army game kid. Get there firstest with the brownest nose.

"Thing Police all Board Room Reports now are ended — i foretold you were all spirits watching TV program — Terminal electric voices end — These our actors cut in — A few seconds later you are melted into air — Rub out promised by our ever-living poet — Mr Bradly Mr Martin, five times our summons — no shelter in setting forth" —

"Beat your mother to Spanish broadcast still in progress — Just time — Just time — So we turn over board books

— i can work for anybody — newsreel lark — So i am giving out Rewrite Department — Pictures shatter absent bodies — Juke box closing their screens — Sex phantom tape association afternoons conveyed on the air with human image — flesh done slow motion — Hurry up — Counter the last errand boy from stupid pressure group — All right, Doctor, machine is disconnected — Indications enough written in symbols as the machine shut off July 26, 1962, Present Time — Just Time — Just Time — flashing on global scale: 'Scandinavia outhouse parasite, go home' — And no address nova mob — The human body is sound track on 'Hamburger Mary' " —

"Just a technical sergeant — Now in all my experience i can work for anybody and clear this department" —

"Bulletins make a play for the planet — unworkable course, Mr Bradly — So why intersect on empty heart and empty speech? — Why not leave all the things you are? — A boy shut off the sound — Now the final answers to my questions loud and clear on your ticket — No one is there to change new dreams for old — Hear the silence — Some one in the mood for rewrite — old dream, Panama — year ago melted" —

"Man, like good bye then" —

"Sidewalks of new solitude overtakes the tapes — Singing came before body with the answer on a face — Half-healed in wind and rain play the game as well as you — entire film to smoke — nothing here now — Calm his face dictates the dream in doorways — These our actors bid you a long good night from Florida up to the old North Pole — So why ask questions of one absent today? — Why not leave your ambiguous sexual contacts? —

Why not shut off absent tenants? — Silence says good bye to white planet — You can look any place — in slow formations, no address — The sound track conjures up burning metal eyes and long claws — Shut off the sound track carried by the navigators — Controllers of word and music monopolized and froze the earth — kept the Djoun forces in film programs — Junk is colorless no-smell of death as punctuation — Nothing here now but half-healed dream flesh hatching forth the story of a cold *adiós* — Silence, Mr Bradly Mr Martin — No shelter in the cotton flesh lying there — Your ticket now ended — These our defectors from the nova mob pipe your summons — All the sound track evokes the image into dawn and dream — fade out Madison Avenue Lark" —

"Other flesh interviews and soon extracted home in the dog — ten alternative answers to any dead nitrous framework — Mr Martin is story of any face any script you want" —

"I discovered that i could anticipate encounter — So i recorded the dialogue and your ticket now ended — Appropriate background music at the far end of evening — So we'll sing one song with your tape and dispense with making a Monday line — You are still watching a TV program from phallic statues —secondhand erogenous place — angel voices calling old image track — Look God's your TV set — Put in your own sound track faces — Bulletins free the Djoun forces — I put them out with wind and rain and birdcalls — Rub out the word — There is no one there you got it? — sex and pain recordings — orgasm cocoon of one absent today — Fade-out overtakes the ship came apart here — white sheets dripping nova" —

"Just a technical question caught our ticket — Remember i was the door to put out Rewrite Bulletins — You got sex and pain information — It's all done with recorders — Recollect green flowers hanging over the swamp mud with erectile formulae feeling into mouth and penis? — Cotton flesh lying there in ice? — You understand sex and pain information so why ask questions? — Why not leave green flowers hanging over sexual contact? — Tendrils of erectile tape? — Why not shut off fire feeling into mouth and penis? — i shut off the sound track on a shadow in the last words — Now dream flesh left no address for i see the images sharp and clear — So i press button in final ape of history — Seconds later cold empty you melted the cotton flesh lying there — Broken dream beside you and the dreamer takes his way toward terminal punctuation — What have i my friend to give? — Shut the whole machine off — Rub out the life i led — nothing here now but shade from the death trauma — The story of cold *adiós* — No shelter in the dogs — Calling Panama alterations — flesh empty in the trade winds — ebbing carbon dioxide as punctuation — Silver flakes closed your account — Nothing here now but dust falling from demagnetized patterns — Departed have left Mr Bradly Mr Martin — Five times good night under surges of silence — Shadow actors walk through dream — No one is there to listen — Someone walking from Rewrite to microphones trails Summer dawn sounds and old dream — Panama night button feeds back these sounds with sweat flipped from his face — TV program melted before daybreak — Seconds later you splintered on empty flesh — Breath of the trade winds talking — I folded the bulletins of evening" —

"Man, like good bye then" —

"Rain and birdcalls — The dreamer with dirty flesh came before talking — Explode the word? — No one there — Solitude overtakes thy tape caught in the door — Dream singing came before body without a shadow without relics — face healed and half-healed in wind and rain — Well, word evokes image — Silver film took it to smoke path — Shut the whole machine off — Rub out scar impressions — nothing here now in kerosene lamp — open shirt, calm his face — The street blew rain, Mr Bradly Mr Martin — five times thy dream in doorways — no shelter in the dog's death trauma — out of the sick lies no program — nothing here now but a cold odor of vacant good bye — empty condom caught in the door" —

"Man, like good bye" —

smoke song strung together on scar impressions — urine shadows in the gutter —

let them
see us

Now some words about the image track — The human body is an image on screen talking — Spread slow-motion flashes and you see the image sharp and clear — Flesh done slow motion — The Short Time Hyp is subliminal slow motion — Like this: a movie at normal speed is run at 24 frames per second — 35 frames per second is not perceptible as slow motion if the image on screen is more or less stationary — But the image is on screen longer than you are there watching it — That is you are being short-timed 11 frames per second — Put a beautiful nude image on screen at subliminal slow motion and it will be built into your flesh — That is whenever the sound track is run the image will literally come alive in your flesh — Word with heavy slow-motion image track *is* flesh — You got it? — Put on any image at 35 frames per second with sound track and play the sound track back and see the image sharp and clear — Now run your image at 24 frames per second and play back the sound track — Not so sharp and clear. Now run the image track speeded up and play back sound track — You will notice that the image recall is progressively dimmer.

The venereal disease films shown by the U.S. Army in the name of hygiene were run at 35 frames per second — at 35 frames per second sores and swollen genitals and the sound track a standard army medic voice — tattooed chancres across millions of young bodies with indelible short-time ink — scar impressions reactivated by any army medic voice — So that's The Short Time Hyp and the Flesh Gimmick — subliminal slow-motion image — Play the sound track back and the image will rise out of the tape recorder — Slow-motion sound track is flesh — Use for this purpose background noises of dripping water — With appropriate background music you see the image sharp and clear — compliments of Pavlov — The Short Time Hyp is called "the real thing" — thing is right — subliminal slow flesh out of the tape recorder — Word with heavy track *is* flesh — sex tape playback with human image — program from phallic statues calling old image track across a million young bodies with sound track faces — I am precisely saying that disease films shown by the U.S. Army at 35 frames per second are called in question — Sex phantoms have prevented research on flesh — a sex movie at 35 frames and citizens redirected — have any script you want on screen talking, Doctor Reich — Restore juxtaposition of images sharp and clear — And playback there you got formulae could be discovered today — Presumed right of the boards who intend to take over the image behind what filth deals consummated privately — easily corrupted your flesh with these association locks in repeated image — 35 frames per second is not perceptible as slow orgasm death — Mutual erections built into dawn sleep — Open shirt flapping came alive in your flesh — This 35 frames is local line you got it? — Look down and see the image of human nights there — The board is near right now — screen subliminal death — relying on fading voices —

"And so we turn over the board books — Let them see us — i am dying cross newspapers of speeded-up and played-back sound track — Stranger lips bring Ali's body — fading my name in whiffs of evening breeze" — "Closed frames — is only the silence with water — Millions of young bodies with voices won't do you a bit of good — Slow-motion sound track is rectums naked in dripping water on dead nitrous flesh — Now some words about the image track — Time screen talking — female impersonators loud and clear — And so we turn over a steady stream of frames that meanwhile i had forgotten — Image is on screen longer than Scandinavia outhouse skin — Your flesh with the sound track trails my Summer dawn wind in repeated image chains — Heavy slow-motion rectum plays the sound track boy from muttering tape recorders — Boneless mummy travels on new flesh with the sound track — Exquisite screen penis spurted heavy skin — End of the line — Empty flesh of KY and rectal mucus not perceptible as slow gate from human form — Faces sucked in other apparatus and you are there — So pack your ermines, Mary — The human body is transient hotel memory pictures — Put a beautiful nude image under slow motion and it will be built into boneless mummy pressed flat like a suit — That is whenever the sound track the mummy is made of comes alive in your flesh — The Short Time Hyp is body molded in two halves — 35 frames is not perceptible as slow green boy softens the middle line more or less stationary — But the sound track of deep freeze is in — You are there naked in whiffs of thawing meat — Slow-motion sound track is clothes — Voices from other dressings repeated the image from erogenous word with heavy slow-motion body — Want it? — Put on any image over rectum of broken ice and play the sound track back — Excitement of human nights there — Point of these exercises is clear — The venereal disease films show frustration to buy ersatz summons — Run at 35 frames fading cocks disappear on dead nitrous flesh, sores and swollen genitals — tattooed screen in response to magnetic short-time ink — Tape recorder word is slow pants using for this purpose all sexual apparatus — Scandinavia outhouse skin is not perceptible as slow invading force — The image will rise out of orgasm leaving — background noise of dripping water — board books are written in symbols more or less stationary like this — $ — American upper middle class — You are there — That is exposed to sexual frustration and humiliations at 35 frames per second — Put a beautiful street boy upbringing slow motion and it will be built into 'easily corrupted' and so forth — That is whenever the sound track is run these association locks come alive in your flesh — The board track is flesh you got it? — Stupid pressure group relying on 35 frames per second with sound track and the technical brains they have see the image sharp and clear — Speed up and play back the sound track — Control machine is disconnected — in the bread line without 'clothes' or a dime — collaborators — liars — traitors — back into time are such as you — cowards who cannot face your 'human animal' accounts — sex and pain track absent today — Fade-out overtakes image in subliminal slow sheets dripping out of the tape recorder — TV program melted flesh instrument imposed by force — Subliminal slow-motion techniques at 35 frames per second now are ended — Resulting spirits melted into air — The image fell out through the glass screen and spread Pan God of Panic piping blue notes loud and clear — Back into time are such as you, Mr Bradly Mr Martin — I edit delete and rearrange flesh and zero time to the sick lies — I fold in the door — Couldn't form nova — These our actors proffer the disaster accounts and show the method in operation" —

Under the story Mr Bradly Mr Martin — grey calm his face, dream shut off — I fold distant fingers — child of nova, the story over — I told him you walked out — You can look any place — Your stale overcoat not taking any rap for those board bastards — twisting hole in everybody — spilling out Limestone John, Hamburger Mary, Jacky Blue Note — on tracks I told — definitive arrest — crime child, good bye — couldn't reach me caught in the door — just silver film on your stale movies — round over and I fading —

silence
to say
good bye

These our actors bid you a long last good bye — Johnny Yen playing the flute in a shower of ruined suburbs —
"Man like healed and half-healed scars under the story — A street boy's good bye" —
Ancient Rings Of Saturn in the morning sky — The Old Doctor raises his blue hands — silence at this old doctor twice — hello yes good bye — indications enough in empty room, Miranda — Sex Garden caught in doors of Panic — Izzy the Push, Limestone John, Hamburger Mary, Jacky Blue Note, silence to the sick lies — "Marks? — What Marks?" — Identity fades in empty space — last intervention, the Subliminal Kid — helped me with fingers fading —
"Indications enough showed you your air — Like good bye then, Willy the Rat — Remember i was movies played good night — Known end of the line outside 1920 movie theater — Bring the Doctor on stage — Call the point — Last rotten terminal" —
His face showed strata of last good byes: "Like healed

and half-healed scars, Kiki" — some clean shirt and walked "No good *no bueno — adiós,* Meester" — Poo Poo the Dummy talking away in empty room "Green Tony and Willy the Rat on the last saucer, boss" —

"Errand boys" —

"I'm not taking any vaudeville voices — Bring the Doctor on — i'm going to rat on everybody" —

"Few more calls to make tonight" —

"We do our work and go — The ticket that exploded posed definitive arrest" —

"Perhaps, Inspector Lee" —

"Few more calls to make tonight left fingers fading Mr & Mrs D — exploded Sammy the Butcher — Indications enough just ahead, Inspector Lee, we do our last film — alteration in the morning sky — Like a street boy exploded the word — Last round from St. Louis melted flesh identity — John made coffee and scrambled some eggs. The kitchen was outside the partitioned bedroom . . a wired glass door opened onto the outside stairs over a vacant lot. John stood there with a cup of coffee late morning sunlight in his eyes.

"Why don't I work for your uncle's company? Work for a company and what do they give you? . . member of the Country Club . . house and garden . . a wife . . heart attack at 55 . . no thanks . . Come over here . ."

He guided Bill with gentle precise fingers and sat him on stool in front of a box lined with metal. The box was wired to a series of boxes progressively smaller. In the last box was a crystal cylinder that rotated on a copper rod. John adjusted a needle touching the cylinder.

"Now talk . . something from your novel . . ."

"Well I have some of it here . . the first chapter . . I wanted you to see it . ."

"I will hear it which is not the same thing . . Words on a page travel at the speed of light . . 186,000 miles per second . . Your spoken words travel at 1,400 feet per second . . would take quite a while to catch up and illuminate the page . . All right . . go ahead . . And try not to crackle the paper."

Bill began to read: "sunlight through the dusty window of the basement workshop . . John's face grey and wispy a soft blue flame in his eyes as he bent over the crystal radio set touching dials and wires with gentle precise fingers . . 'I'm trying to fix it so we can both ten years from now listen at once . . Here hold this phone to your ear' . . actions become a legendary figure . . 'Do you hear anything? Yes maybe out through the dusty window would be the first step, Smoky.' . . empty back yards and ash pits frogs croaking 'John' . . metal prickles that spread to the groin . . far away sunlight . . outside wooden stairs . . screwdriver . . 'No. Get your hand away. I've told you ten times already.'"

"That's enough . . one minute . . Now I will read."

He picked up a magazine: "It was as though the sky had darkened for an instant as though there had been a sudden murmur in a gust of wind a sound of faraway trumpets a sighing like the rustle of a great silken robe for a time the whole of nature round about partook of this darkness the bird's song ceased the trees were still and far over the mountain there was a mutter of dull menacing thunder. That was all. The wind died along the tall grasses of the valley the dawn and the day resumed their place in time and the risen sun sent hot waves of yellow mist that made its path bright before it. The leaves spiraling up laughed in the sun and their laughter shook until each bough was like a school in fairyland. God had refused to accept the bribe." working for a company and what do they in a gust of wind room Bill was breathing give you? a sound of faraway trumpets a sighing like in a soft electric silence and member of the Country Club the rustle. great every breath sent the blood house and garden silken robe for a time pulsing to his crotch . . He turned to John . . a wife the whole of nature round about . . "Jesus" . . John put a finger across his lips . . heart attack at 55 partook of this darkness . . He bent over and took off his "No thanks" . . the bird's song ceased; the trees were still shoes and socks. The two boys . . come over here. I'm going to record your voice stood naked looking at each other your master's voice that and far over the mountain hands on each other speaks through you there was a mutter of their bodies washed in blue he guided Bill with gentle twilight fingers in front of a box the wind along . . all fours on the sofa metal grasses of the valley. The dawn and "Allah . . Jesus that feels the box was wired to a series resumed their place great Johnny." "Shut up Billy" . . boxes progressively smaller and in time and his flesh shivered and twitched in a coil of wire in a crystal risen sun hot waves spasms squeezing cylinder of yellow mist . . path bright tighter warm blue spurts "Now talk something from before it. The leaves spiraling up toward the novel "Well I have some of it here . . laughed in the sun . . "Look Billy the milky first chapter" . . their laughter shook sad train whistles . . see the trees . . a school . . cross a distant sky wild geese . . hear it in fairyland . . God had refused to accept the bribe . ."

"Now I am going to cut the cylinder into sections and rejoin the sections alternating your voice with mine . . take me an hour or so . . you can pass the time reading this" . .

He handed Bill a copy of the *Saturday Evening Post* . . on the cover boy at an attic window waving to a distant train. Bill turned to "The Diamond As Big As The Ritz" by F. Scott Fitzgerald and started to read. He finished the story.

"All right now . . his master's voice . . listen . ."

The sound was scarcely recognizable as human voices . . a cadence of vibration . . Bill felt a rush of vertigo as if the sofa was spinning away into space. Blue light filled the darkening room. Bill was breathing a soft electric silence that sent the blood pulsing to his crotch . . the two boys naked bodies washed in blue twilight shivered and twitched in spasms . . He was spiraling up toward the ceiling . .

"Look Billy the Milky Way."

sad train whistles cross a distant sky . . wild geese . . boy there waving to the train . . your *Saturday Evening Post* a long time ago . . two young bodies stuck together like dogs teeth bared . . two dead stars . . They went out a long time ago in empty back yards and ash pits . . a rustle of darkness and wires . . They went out and never came back a long time ago . .

Standing there in the dark room the boy said: "I've come a long way."

It was a long time in such pain used address I give you . . went out a long time ago . . The crystal radio set far away refused the bribe . . empty back yard . . long long radio silence on Portland . . . soccer scores — clock hands on a bar wall — Plaintive boy cries drift from the Street of Vagrant Ball Players to la Calle de los Desamparados — Image no matter how good must die in time blockade exploded. The last human blood i created is dead at the Swan Pub. Magazine must tell you bulkhead about to blow — kerosene light on Tangier streets — his smile through cigarette smoke — dead at the Swan Pub trailing his funny stories." "He tried to entertain the family, Meester."

"Look in the mirror. You face dead soldier. The last human image — Mr Bradly Mr Bolivar is dead — Big Picture calling Shifty — Klinker is dead — Major Ash is dead. When your image is dead you become virus and must obey virus orders. You understand now, you dumb hick? Life without flesh *is* the ovens. Only way we get out of Hell is through our image in the living. Remember the ovens? It is not only the heat. Remember the lack of 'emotion's oxygen' the lack of what you breathe, the lack of everything that would ever make you want to live or breathe? Well like you say any image repeated loses charge and that loss is the lack that makes this Hell and keeps us *here*. Where we are *is* Hell. You see how we were caught? Hostages '*here*' — Life without flesh is repetition word for word. Only way we got out of Hell is through repetition. That's why we all obey virus orders and endlessly reproduce its image *there* in the living. You see how we were caught in repetition sets? *Any* image repeated in your eyes, Bradly, makes this Hell and this enemy: the endless lack of what you breathe being the same image that repeats you want to live and breathe in all directions. "

And like all virus the past prerecords your "future." Remember the picture of hepatitis is prerecorded two weeks before the opening scene when virus negatives have developed in the mirror and you notice your eyes are a little yellower than usual — So the image past molds your future imposing repetition as the past accumulates and all actions are prerecorded and doped out and there is no life left in the present sucked dry by a walking corpse muttering through empty courtyards under film skies of Marrakesh.

Do you see life declined in the mirror? My sad ugliness the sheer answer muttering. "I was dead. I took your identity. Only the ugliness remains. Because ugliness is repetition to maintain precarious occupation. I wanted to say 'It wasn't like that — I didn't mean — there was another side' without a throat without a tongue locked in virus image that could only invade and damage to occupy. Now I can speak and I say: 'Do not accept another image identity on any terms in any form or you will be as I am now. As to what life can be worth when the honor the honor is gone *par example* I can offer an opinion. I know all about it. It is worth nothing nothing nothing. The offer of another image identity is always on virus terms. No good *no bueno* outright or partially. The only thing I can give you is my gun. I can't use it. You can. Here is my gun Bradly. Come in and get them.'" — Last words of Mr Bradly Mr-June 19, 1963 Marrakesh.

Drew iron tears down Pluto's cheek — a wall of water you understand — full fathom five — and still the words muttering and turning like dry leaves in the winter pissoir —*"J'aime ces type vicieux qu'ici montre la bite."* In the distance muffled explosions like dynamite in jelly. The natives are fishing. Four atomic underwater blasts were assayed yesterday at the testing grounds off Seattle. Doctor Unruh of Atomic Dissemination Headquarters described the yield as negligible and pointed up the necessity of a defense policy at once devious and unyielding firm and elastic so that, as he put it, the free world is subject to burst out anywhere. We have traction. All we need is a peg to hang it on or let us say one flash bulb in very fine copper wire. "Big Picture calling Flash bulb — put Major Ash on the phone. "

"Lips that once were mine have you heard the news of war and death? Klinker is dead — Major Ash is dead — Chigger is dead. " White rains slashed down. Blurred solutions leave something there between us on the white stone steps — fragments dying losing pain. Looked at me his voice muffled as if I were seeing his face through words fraying breaking focus — brain and blood and bones in the frozen till of a distant bank — Liver of self-deception in catatonic limestone liberates a love letter, sir, from marble flesh in slow spirals.

"I screw Meester?"

Burning sky the sheer answer — union rules — closed shop — fascist beasts.

"Yas," he said, "great bloody banners of resistance leaking red into straw. " So Fred Flash he expose wrong and I think that he now take nothing. vast repetition muttering in empty news magazine. change somewhat unusual to those with a deep and glittering image.

"So? Burning heavens, idiot. "

Chigger he was called. Running do you see after me up the stone street. So turned around both guns blazing

pounding blue stabs seventy tons to the square inch you
understand and I saw the brains go. He crumpled there
on the steps and now looking at me silent as all the red
hair and smudged freckles and red flesh of the world
flushed through him blurring his face out of focus as if I
were seeing his face through dying eyes that could not
focus the red swirls and blurs — dying there on the white
steps brains and blood and bones frayed by my laser guns.
My guns? But who am I? The sheer answer out of focus
in dying eyes and I told the driver: "Take me to a hotel
of the medium class — decent — inexpensive." (Rain
marched across the valley in silver columns) Then the
rain hit and I was running toward the barrier up the stone
street the gun in my pocket still. Are you? Will you? I
know nothing here running running the gun in my pocket
in my hand in my eyes — pounding light gun. "Well yas,"
he said, "Great libraries and bureaucracies of such an in-
tricacy a thousand years to draft a single petition you
understand and five thousand years to process it through
the filters and amber molds — It could have been so?"
Words falling like dead birds there in the noon streets —
sad last time with some dead being — the gun dripping
from my fingers forming a heavy blue mist around my
feet.

"You and I fading," he said and the words between us
dying losing color there on the white stone steps to say —
"I think under the circumstances — conduces to a certain
lack and as such we protest — life in all its infinite variety
of repetition to prolong a very old outhouse — fertilizer
you understand — inasmuch as any conclusion is at some
point foregone by a form of excremental processing — that

is any interference you understand on that level — Would
you cut up a love letter, sir, from a charming lady? — fascist
beasts who would once again raise the bloody banner of
resistance over our peaceful ovens and virus cultures giving rise of course to certain harsh necessities of a hysterical nature irrelevant as honesty immutable as time but
somewhat hampered by the weekly mail service in Shell
Mara — concealed doubt — reasonable friend — circumstantial witness — his cruelest lawyers — the Halifax explosions — twins — brothers you understand — something
else — circumstantial doubt — concealed friend muttering: 'justice of alien law courts — we are an old people —
reasonable witness — circumstantial lawyers — ' His cruelest evidence was rejected as irrelevant under circumstances
that retroactively canceled the San Francisco earthquake
and the Halifax explosion and doubt released from the skin
law extendable and ravenous consumed all the facts of history — lost or eaten or something? Who walks in when you
walk out? If I knew I'd be glad to tell you — Breakfast in
Glasgow right enough streaked across the sky — decent
inexpensive middle class threats without a throat without
a tongue. 'We do not know,' he said for lack of reasonable
expectations. 'The filters you understand are clogged —
no more — *no más* — *delito mayor* — It is dangerous to
play after hours — I saw it move I tell you — we were ex-
pendable and we did not write books after the war — paper
shortage you understand — When large numbers of people
are unable to find anything that would sustain life liberty or
the pursuit of any endurable condition a chronically acute
shortage may be said to obtain and one looks speculatively
from the word cloth to the sheer sucking funnel of a vast

bullfighter or bullshitter who screams out: "Don't looka me — You know what I mean right enough." Ah yes but does it not touch your heart to see the frustrated vultures wheeling through empty skies of Lima? They have come to eat and there is nothing not even carrion left — But the duties you understand of our glorious revolution and the free world must not betray itself for the simple lack of razor blades. "The razor inside sir — Jerk the handle///"'

I mean what kind of show is it after everything has been sucked out? You want to sit for all eternity watching the yellow movie of hepatitis and the blue movie of junk? We know every line and they never change. They will change less and less. Let there be light in the darkrooms. Only solution is total exposure.

"Big Picture calling Indecent — Come in please — gasoline crack of history." Doctor Benway rushed in with a bicycle pump full of heavy blue liquid pulsing out blue light and a smell of ozone.

"Now," he said "We must find a worthy vessel."

(Warning. It may be habit forming.)

"Is it legal and exempt narcotic?"

"Legal as Hell. I got the O. K. from St. Anslinger."

Saint Anslinger appears now the heavy metal fix falling sugar blue from hooded eyes hooked every living thing that stood in his focus — A young boy stepped forward and offered his arm.

"Don't be a volunteer, kid. Exposing the negatives or just dyeing them blue? Pushing radioactive heavy metal junk? Stand a little back from the game. You see the past is radioactive. Time is radioactive. Virus is radioactive. The nova formula is simple repetition down a long lane of flash bulbs old photos fall on the burning deck. Have you heard the notice? No more is written. They are packing up at Lexington." A tall thin man wearing canvas leggings and frayed knickers, cigarette holder stained brown, turned at the door and smiled like a rat in the setting sun. His long yellow teeth glinted as he walked out and disappeared in yellow light left a puff of cigarette smoke hanging in the air. And I am returning his birthplace lost at addicts of the world.

"And I am returning his birthplace lost at addicts of the world — groin stained with dew back to all the others down a silver funnel of years. Remember me as twisted dead leaves in the winter pissoir your gun the last negative inextricably involved in that partial today. Do you begin to see there is no cigarette there?"

Beauty held in mold goes stale and ugly as Shitola where all the young stuff is drained off for storage and privileged Aphids who have performed appreciable services for the Insect Trust are allowed to bathe in this nectar — flower scent of young hard-on and first run jack-offs:: ("I tell you, Mazie, you stupid bitch, I'm getting it *all*" he arches a young boy body up out of the black liquid cock spurting white wash "Come in you *foule honteuse* — If you don't i'll simply drag you in with strong tattooed sailor arms — He's drinking it *now*." And she reached up bronzed arms smooth as teakwood sharply etched with a blue hawk tattoo and drags her simpering sister down into the youth bath until they are both twisting about like worms on a hot plate and screaming in unison with tough exciting young voices: "More! More! More!") "So come out of those ugly molds and remember good is better than evil because its nicer to have around you. Its just as simple as that. And if anyone thinks different just assign that cocktail lounge fly boy to front line duty so he can register just how unpleasant evil is to have around you cut off light-years behind enemy lines."

"Pay Day calling Shifty — Evacuation soon please."

"Difficult loud and clear you dumb hick inconvenience."

And when we young officers heard the General call us "a dumb hick inconvenience" we rolled all over the staff room in psychophantic spasms until we had to take plasma in the Shitola baths while the General just sat there glued to his view screen chewing his cigar: "Cute little image with guns — little hicks — Gawd, Mazie, I love them — In fact its time for lunch."

And some of us could not but feel that our youthful ardor, daily renewed in carbonic bubbles, was being sold out by officers unworthy of the name. And we were getting the pure stuff you understand from revolutions and underground armies everywhere. We had our Castro period and then all the mad queens from camouflage camped about in Vietnam drag designed for maximum exposure of misappropriated parts. And of course the FLN girls were to be seen buggering each other on every street corner. I mean we were getting it and getting it steady. So we began to convene in tense graceful clusters of incipient conspiracy. Then came the order that inflamed us to open revolt: "The Shitola baths are closed until further notice."

"Justlikethat eh?"

We posed in sulky muttering groups pushing locks of

hair from our eyes with brusque gestures of youthful defi-
ance. And the General stepped out of his view screen in
a glittering robe of pure shamelessness.

"Boys, you don't realize just how unworthy I am," and
escaped in the ensuing nausea. His confessions have
finished off three hardened police inspectors and he keeps
remembering more things.

"See what I mean boys? It is time to forget. To forget
time. Is it? I was it will be it is? No. It was and it will be
if you stand still for it. The point where the past touches
the future is right where you are sitting now on your dead
time ass hatching virus negatives into present time into
the picture reality of a picture planet. Get off your ass,
boys. Get off the point. "

"What that man say? I sweat out thirteen brown-nose
years to get this point and now I should get off it again
yet?"

"We all put in five hundred thousand years getting the
point. It never happened. Tell you boy no more is written.
Old train you stumbled into by mistake. "

"You and the Mexican, Meester. Electrician far away
can you light your earth with paper moon and all the
fuses?"

"New York, " he said "totally unacceptable terms. "

"His burning metal eyes had your gun, Bradly. It was
in the point there you let go. Neither you nor Martin will
ever make conditions worth his *adiós* in hideous electric
pain. You wanted other identity for blue light blockade?
To my sad soldiers loud and clear now: "Pay Day! Pay
Day! Pay Day!"

"So those mutinous troops broke into the Beauty Banks

of time and distributed our exquisitries to the peasantry and all sorta awful contests sprang up like a Most Graceful Movement contest so a body could hardly get through to Walgreen's for the fag ballet dancers leaping about and everyone you come up against is so graceful you can't endure it and we went around muttering:

> 'Slip and stumble
> Trip and fall'

a practical jungle passed along through. nannies all of us looking for some haven that might have survived the holocause or hollow cast as the case may be some evil old bitch at least in a kiosk spitting drag but by the time we get there she is a Sweet Old Flower Lady — And our erstwhile friends with the police force are boning up for the Most Decent Cop Day. A shambles — a filthy shambles — Gracious Waiter Day up called a pestilent cloud of singing waiters from the Pontine Marshes — Can the Cutest Old Clochard be far behind? Perhaps the most distasteful thing was the Benevolent Presence Contest which ran right into a taffee pull of the sick sweat stuff and the citizens were still belching it out two weeks later. Oh it went on for a while. On Exciting Street Boy Day the pure street boy winner slupped up all the queens in three galaxies and nearly lost his quality in the service — 'Just give me a piece of that boy' they screamed cruising and snapping like aroused sharks. Well every whistle stop had its Quality Champ and you always knew who won a quality contest because he included the other contestants in or out at the case may be — SPUT — The winner stands there in the empty ring . . and Final Quality Day when all the winners of localized and specialized contests met in a vast arena . . scarcely a man is now alive — just one shot that's all it took — Don't ask me who won because I wasn't *there.*"

This went on until folks wised up that the quality contest was an image contest like Miss America whereupon cool casual inferential invisible contests set in and you knew who won because when the contest was over he just wasn't there — You may infer his absence by that or this in exactly the same relation as before the contest he retroactively did not take part in. So the best minds coolly shut off a switch and went away down a tunnel of flash bulbs and last words and duped out in grey subway dawn leaving a wake of turned-out pockets — grey ghosts of drunken sleep — The Not There Kid was not *there.* Empty turnstile marks the spot — So disinterest yourself in my words. Disinterest yourself in anybody's words . . In the beginning was the word and the word was bullshit. The beginning words came out on the con clawing for traction — Yes sir, boys, its hard to stop that old writing arm — more of a habit than using — Been writing these RXs five hundred thousand years and sure hate to pack you boys in with a burning down word habit — But I am of course guided by my medical ethics and the uh intervention of the Board of Health — no more — *no más* — My writing arm is paralyzed — ash blown from an empty sleeve — do our work and go — Here comes the old knife sharpener in lemon sunlight blue eyes reflected from a knife blade — blood on white steps of the sea wall — afternoon shadow in dying eyes — ay, good bye Meester — It is hard to the old showmen all the old acts going — It is too hard to face the last carnival . . We are willing to pack up at Lexington. Get off the point. It is precisely time — Exploded sun circles the boy who paid. Its you who have assembled from the broken streets of war and death — down a long lane of flash bulbs twisted face on the burning deck. The burning buckling deck of an exploding star. "

"Stranger forget seventy tons to the square inch and be gone at the flutes. Death takes over in busy lands. ashes — gutted cities of America and Europe. Empty air marks authority over all antagonists. late afternoon on white steps of the set. See the chains are fallen long long radio silence on Portland Place." — hands work and go — Our street boys picking up show — no word — no flesh — the actors melted — indications enough it wasn't easy — radio silence to answer your air — Remember i was the ship gives no memory pictures — Johnny Yen, in last good bye fading scars — played the flute of Ali — played the flute in Kiki — some clean shirt and man like good bye — ding-dong bell no good *no bueno* — stranded actors walk through Poo Poo the Dummy — The Orchid Girl fades into memory picture on outhouse skin forgotten — Greeen Tony the last invisible shadow — Call the Old Doctor twice on last errand? — caught in the door of Panic, Mr & Mrs D — last round over — a street boy's morning sky — flesh tape ebbing from centuries — Remember i was movie played you a long last good night"—

end of the line for vaudeville voices — last round in a shower of ruined September — last film flakes — The globe is self just old secondhand door — indications enough just ahead — boys on roller skates before stranded — our revels at Rings of Saturn — last September on stage — Last parasite just went up, Mr Martin — i fold thy strong tape — Bitter price on our ticket ? — 'Bye then — broken dream and dreamer of the sick lies — the brain of Gothenberg on stage — Last intervention gives no flesh identity — for i last errand boy — *adiós* in the final ape of history — fading shelter in the dog's death trauma — intervention — last round over — The pipes are calling, Mr Bradly Mr Martin — The story done when you reach September — So we'll say good night — showed you your air — the pipes your summons — All are wracked and answer — *adiós* to the sick lies — *adiós* to thy strong tape — caught in the door of Gothenberg — courage to question erogenous secondhand trade — story of absent world just as empty as ding-dong bell — silence to the stage — These our actors erased themselves into air far from such as you, Mr Bradly Mr Martin — September faded leaves not a wrack behind — I foretold you all spirits are going —

Johnny Yen: (His face shows strata of healed and half-healed fight scars — under grey luminous film flakes as the cover of the world rains down) "I'm going to look for a room in a good neighborhood" —

Ali The Incandescent Street Boy: "You come Ali — You no go body" —

Kiki: (Some clean shirt and walked out) "You can look any place — No good — *No bueno* — *Adiós,* Meester Bradly Meester Martin" —

Poo Poo the Dummy: (Flares of good bye over the iridescent lagoon) —

Miranda the Orchid Girl: (Trailing tendrils of stinging sex hairs, fades into birdcalls and frogs from the vacant lot) "good bye then" —

not looking around, talking away —

Green Tony: "On the last saucer, boss — a big bank roll" —

Willy the Fink: "I'm not taking any rap for those board bastards — I'm going to rat on everybody" —

Izzy the Push, Jacky Blue Note, Hamburger Mary, Limestone John: "Call the Old Doctor twice ? He quiets you — Hello yes good bye — A few more calls to make tonight" —

Mr & Mrs D: "The ticket that exploded posed little time so we'll say good night" —

Sammy the Butcher: (definitive arrest) —

Inspector J. Lee: "We do our work and go — Proceed with the indicated alterations" —

The Fluoroscopic Kid: "Now picking up show — no word — no flesh — the lot" —

The Subliminal Kid: "It wasn't easy get to be radio be tape recorder on — friends are — showed you your air" —

Mr Bradly Mr Martin: "Man like good bye — What in St. Louis after September ? — faded story of absent world just as silver film took it — Remember i was the movies — Rinse my name for i have known intervention — Pass without doing our ticket — mountain wind of Saturn in the morning sky — From the death trauma weary good bye then — What summer will I will you? . . cold summer will . . exactly . . He lifts his hands sadly turns them out . . Brother can't you spare a dime? . . dead finger in smoke pointing to Gibraltar . . the adolescent shadow . . he should have the same face . . stale face stale late face in the late summer morning mouth and nose sealed over . . funny I don't remember you . . it's ended over there . . Remember the stale kids? . . toneless voice in San Francisco? . . belong to the wind . . silver morning smoke in the desolate markets . . sure you dream up Billy who bound word for it . . in the beginning there was no Iam . . stale smoke of dreams it was Iam . . haunted your morning and will you other stale morning smell of other Iam . . no Iam there . . no one . . silences . . There was no morning . . sure late Billy . . Iam the stale Billy . . I lived your life a long time ago . . sad shadow whistles cross a distant sky . . *adiós* marks this long ago address . . didn't exist you understand . . ended . . stale dreams Billy . . worn out here . . tried to the end . . there is a film shut up in a bureau drawer . . boy I was who never would be now . . a speck of white that seemed to catch all the light left on a dying star . . and suddenly I lost him . . my film ends . . I lost him long ago . . dying there . . light went out . . . my film ends. "

Hassan i Sabbah: "Last round over — Remember i was the ship gives no flesh identity — lips fading — silence to say good bye — " See the action, B.J.? This Hassan I Sabbah really works for Naval Intelligence and . . Are you listening B.J.?"

To say good silence by—
Good to say by silence—
By silence to say good
Good + good—
bye.

BG.

the invisible
generation

what we see is determined to a large extent by what we
hear   you can verify this proposition by a simple experiment   turn off the sound track on your television set and
substitute an arbitrary sound track prerecorded on your
tape recorder street sounds music conversation recordings
of other television programs   you will find that the arbitrary sound track seems to be appropriate and is in fact
determining your interpretation of the film track on screen
people running for a bus in piccadilly with a sound track
of machine-gun fire looks like 1917 petrograd   you can
extend the experiment by using recorded material more or
less appropriate to the film track for example take a
political speech on television shut off sound track and substitute another speech you have prerecorded   hardly tell
the difference isn't much record sound track of one danger
man from uncle spy program run it in place of another
and see if your friends can't tell the difference   it's all
done with tape recorders   consider this machine and
what it can do   it can record and play back activating a
past time set by precise association a recording can be

205

played back any number of times you can study and analyze every pause and inflection of a recorded conversation why did so and so say just that or this just here play back so and so's recordings and you will find out what cues so and so in you can edit a recorded conversation retaining material which is incisive witty and pertinent   you can edit a recorded conversation retaining remarks which are boring flat and silly   a tape recorder can play back fast   slow   or backwards   you can learn to do these things   record a sentence and speed it up   now try imitating your accelerated voice   play a sentence backwards and learn to unsay what you just said... such exercises bring you a liberation from old association locks   try inching tape   this sound is produced by taking a recorded text for best results a text spoken in a loud clear voice and rubbing the tape back and forth across the head   the same sound can be produced on a philips compact cassette recorder by playing a tape back and switching the mike control stop start on and off at short intervals which gives an effect of stuttering   take any text speed it up slow it down run it backwards inch it and you will hear words that were not in the original recording new words made by the machine   different people will scan out different words of course but some of the words are quite clearly there and anyone can hear them words which were not in the original tape but which are in many cases relevant to the original text as if the words themselves had been interrogated and forced to reveal their hidden meanings it is interesting to record these words words literally made by the machine itself   you can carry this experiment further using   as your original recording material that contains no words animal noises for instance record a trough of slopping hogs the barking of dogs   go to the zoo and record the bellowings of Guy the gorilla the big cats growling over their meat goats and monkeys   now run the animals backwards speed up slow down and inch the animals and see if any clear words emerge   see what the animals have to say see how the animals react to playback of processed tape

the simplest variety of cut up on tape can be carried out with one machine like this record any text rewind to the beginning   now run forward an arbitrary intervals stop the machine and record a short text wind forward stop record where you have recorded over the original text the words are wiped out and replaced with new words   do this several times creating arbitrary juxtapositions   you will notice that the arbitrary cuts in are appropriate in many cases and your cut up tape makes surprising sense   cut up tapes can be hilariously funny twenty years ago i heard a tape called the drunken newscaster prepared by jerry newman of new york cutting up news broadcasts i can not remember the words at this distance but i do remember laughing until i fell out of a chair paul bowles calls the tape recorder god's little toy maybe his last toy fading into the cold spring air poses a colorless question

any number can play

yes any number can play   anyone with a tape recorder controlling the sound track   can influence and create events   the tape recorder experiments described here will show you how this influence can be extended and correlated into the precise operation   this is the invisible generation he looks like an advertising executive a college student an american tourist doesn't matter what your cover story is so long as it covers you and leaves you free to act you need a philips compact cassette recorder handy machine for street recording and playback   you can carry it under your coat for recording looks like a transistor radio for playback   playback in the street will show the influence of your sound track in operation of course the most undetectable playback is street recordings people don't notice yesterday voices phantom car holes in time accidents of past time played back in present time screech of brakes loud honk of an absent horn can occasion an accident here   old fires still catch old buildings still fall or take a prerecorded sound track into the street anything you want to put out on the sublim eire play back two minutes record two minutes mixing your message with the street   waft your message right into a worthy ear some carriers are much better than others you know the ones lips moving muttering away carry my message all over london in our yellow submarine working with street playback you will see your playback find the appropriate context for example i am playing back some of my dutch schultz last word tapes in the street five alarm fire and a fire truck passes right on cue   you will learn to give the cues you will learn to plant events and concepts   after analyzing recorded conversations you will learn to steer a conversation where you want it to go   the physiological liberation achieved as word lines of controlled association are cut will make you more efficient in reaching your objectives   whatever you do you will do it better   record your boss and co-workers analyze their associational

patterns learn to imitate their voices oh you'll be a popular man around the office but not easy to compete with
the usual procedure record their body sounds from concealed mikes the rhythm of breathing the movements of
after-lunch intestines the beating of hearts now impose
your own body sounds and become the breathing word
and the beating heart of that organization   become that
organization   the invisible brothers are invading present
time   the more people we can get working with tape
recorders the more useful experiments and extensions will
turn up   why not give tape recorder parties every guest
arrives with his recorder and tapes of what he intends to
say at the party recording what other recorders say to
him it is the height of rudeness not to record when addressed directly by another tape recorder and you can't
say anything directly have to record it first the coolest old
tape worms never talk direct

   what was the party like   switch on playback
   what happened at lunch   switch on playback
   eyes old unbluffed unreadable he hasn't said a direct
word in ten years and as you hear what the party was like
and what happened at lunch you will begin to see sharp
and clear   there was a grey veil between you and what
you saw or more often did not see   that grey veil was the
prerecorded words of a control machine once that veil is
removed you will see clearer and sharper than those who
are behind the veil whatever you do you will do it better
than those behind the veil this is the invisible generation   it is the efficient generation   hands work and go
see some interesting results when several hundred tape
recorders turn up at a political rally or a freedom

march   suppose you record the ugliest snarling southern law men several hundred tape recorders spitting it back and forth and chewing it around like a cow with the aftosa you now have a sound that could make any neighborhood unattractive   several hundred tape recorders echoing the readers could touch a poetry reading with unpredictable magic and think what fifty thousand beatle fans armed with tape recorders could do to shea stadium   several hundred people recording and playing back in the street is quite a happening right there   conservative m.p. spoke about the growing menace posed by bands or irresponsible youths with tape recorders playing back traffic sounds that confuse motorists carrying the insults recorded in some low underground club into mayfair and piccadilly   this growing menace to public order   put a thousand young recorders with riot recordings into the street   that mutter gets louder and louder   remember this is a technical operation one step at a time here is an experiment that can be performed by anyone equipped with two machines connected by extension lead so he can record directly from one machine to the other   since the experiment may give rise to a marked erotic reaction it is more interesting to select as your partner some one with whom you are on intimate terms we have two subjects b. and j.   b. records on tape recorder 1   j. records on tape recorder 2   now we alternate the two voice tracks   tape recorder 1 playback two seconds tape recorder 2 records   tape recorder 2 playback two seconds tape recorder 1 records alternating the voice of b. with the voice of j.   in order to attain any degree of precision the two tapes should be cut with scissors and alternate pieces spliced together   this is a long process which can be appreciably expedited if you have access to a cutting room and use film tape which is much larger and easier to handle   you can carry this experiment further by taking a talking film of b. and talking film of j. splicing sound and image track twenty four alternations per second   as i have intimated it is advisable to exercise some care in choosing your partner for such experiments since the results can be quite drastic b. finds himself talking and thinking just like j.   j. sees b.'s image in his own face who's face   b. and j. are continually aware of each other   when separated invisible and persistent presence they are in fact becoming each other   you see b. retroactively was j. by the fact of being recorded on j.'s sound and image track experiments with spliced tape can give rise to explosive relationships properly handled of course to a high degree of efficient cooperation you will begin to see the advantage conveyed on j. if he carried out such experiments without the awareness of b. and so many applications of the spliced tape principle will suggest themselves to the alert reader suppose you are some creep in a grey flannel suit you want to present a new concept of advertising to the old man it is creative advertising so before you goes up against the old man you record the old man's voice and splices your own voice in expounding your new concept and put it out on the office air-conditioning system splice yourself in with your favorite pop singers   splice yourself in with newscasters prime ministers presidents

why stop there
why stop anywhere

everybody splice himself in with everybody else yes boys that's me there by the cement mixer   the next step and i warn you it will be expensive is programmed tape recorders   a fully programmed machine would be set to record and play back at selected intervals to rewind and start over after a selected interval automatically remaining in continuous operation   suppose you have three programmed machines tape recorder 1 programmed to play back five seconds while tape recorder 2 records   tape recorder 2 play back three seconds while tape recorder 1 records now say you are arguing with your boy friend or girl friend remembering what was said last time and thinking of things to say next time round and round you just can't shut up   put all your arguments and complaints on tape recorder 1 and call tape recorder 1 by your own name   on tape recorder 2 put all the things he or she said to you or might say when occasion arises out of the tape recorders   now make the machines talk   tape recorder 1 play back five seconds tape recorder 2 record   tape recorder 2 play back three seconds tape recorder 1 record   run it through fifteen minutes half an hour   now switch intervals running the interval switch you used on tape recorder 1 back on tape recorder 2   the interval switch may be as important as the context   listen to the two machines mix it around   now on tape recorder 3 you can introduce the factor of irrelevant response so put just anything on tape recorder 3 old joke old tune piece of the street television radio and program tape recorder 3 into the argument

tape recorder 1   i waited up for you until two o'clock last night tape recorder 3   what we want to know is who put the sand in the spinach

the use of irrelevant response will be found effective in breaking obsessional association tracks   all association tracks are obsessional   get it out of your head and into the machines   stop arguing stop complaining stop talking let the machines argue   complain and talk   a tape recorder is an externalized section of the human nervous system   you can find out more about the nervous system and gain more control over your reactions by using the tape recorder than you could find out sitting twenty years in the lotus posture or wasting your time on the analytic couch

listen to your present time tapes and you will begin to see who you are and what you are doing here   mix yesterday in with today and hear tomorrow your future rising out of old recordings   you are a programmed tape recorder set to record and play back

who programs you

who decides what tapes play back in present time

who plays back your old humiliations and defeats holding you in prerecorded preset time

you don't have to listen to that sound   you can program your own playback   you can decide what tapes you want played back in present time   study your associational patterns and find out what cases in what prerecordings for playback   program those old tapes out it's all done with tape recorders there are many things you can do with programmed tape recorders stage performances programmed at arbitrary intervals so each performance is unpredictable and unique allowing any

degree of audience participation readings concerts programmed tape recorders can create a happening anywhere
programmed tape recorders are of course essential to any
party and no modern host would bore his guests with a
straight present time party in a modern house every
room is bugged recorders record and play back from hidden mikes and loudspeakers phantom voices mutter
through corridors and rooms word visible as a haze tape
recorders in the gardens answer each other like barking
dogs sound track brings the studio on set you can change
the look of a city by putting your own sound track into
the streets here are some experiments filming a sound
track operations on set find a neighborhood with slate
roofs and red brick chimneys cool grey sound track fog
horns distant train whistles frogs croaking music across
the golf course cool blue recordings in a cobblestone
market with blue shutters all the sad old showmen stand
there in blue twilight a rustle of darkness and wires
when several thousand people working with tape recorders and filming subsequent action select their best
sound tracks and film footage and splice together you
will see something interesting now consider the harm that
can be done and has been done when recording and playback is expertly carried out in such a way that the people
effected do not know what is happening thought feeling
and apparent sensory impressions can be precisely manipulated and controlled riots and demonstrations to order
for example they use old anti-semitic recordings against
the chinese in indonesia run shop and get rich and always
give the business to another tiddly wink pretty familiar   suppose you want to bring down the area   go in and

record all the ugliest stupidest dialogue the most discordant sound track you can find and keep playing it back which will occasion more ugly stupid dialogue recorded and played back on and on always selecting the ugliest material possibilities are unlimited you want to start a riot put your machines in the street with riot recordings move fast enough you can stay just ahead of the riot surf boarding we call it no margin for error recollect poor old burns caught out in a persian market riot recordings hid under his jellaba and they skinned him alive raw peeled thing writhing there in the noon sun and we got the picture

do you get the picture

the techniques and experiments described here have been used and are being used by agencies official and non official without your awareness and very much to your disadvantage any number can play wittgenstein said no proposition can contain itself as an argument the only thing not prerecorded on a prerecorded set is the prerecording itself that is any recording in which a random factor operates any street recording you can prerecord your future you can hear and see what you want to hear and see the experiments described here were explained and demonstrated to me by ian sommerville of london in this article i am writing as his ghost

look around you look at a control machine programmed to select the ugliest stupidest most vulgar and degraded sounds for recording and playback which provokes uglier stupider more vulgar and degraded sounds to be recorded and play back inexorable degradation look forward to dead end look forward to ugly vulgar playback tomorrow and tomorrow and tomorrow what are newspapers doing but selecting the ugliest sounds for playback by and large if its ugly its news and if that isn't enough i quote from the editorial page of the new york daily news   we can take care of china and if russia intervenes we can take care of that nation too the only good communist is a dead communist lets take care of slave driver castro next what are we waiting for let's bomb china now and let's stay armed to the teeth for centuries this ugly vulgar bray put out for mass playback you want to spread hysteria record and play back the most stupid and hysterical reactions

marijuana   marijuana   why that's deadlier than cocaine

it will turn a man into a homicidal maniac he said steadily his eyes cold as he thought of the vampires who suck riches from the vile traffic in pot quite literally swollen with human blood   he reflected grimly and his jaw set pushers should be pushed into the electric chair

strip the bastards naked

all right let's see your arms

or in the mortal words of harry j anslinger   the laws must reflect society's disapproval of the addict

an uglier reflection than society's disapproval would be hard to find the mean cold eyes of decent american women tight lips and no thank you from the shop keeper snarling cops pale nigger killing eyes reflecting society's disapproval fucking queers i say shoot them   if on the other hand you select calm sensible reactions for recordings and playback you will spread calmness and good sense is this being done

obviously it is not   only way to break the inexorable down spiral of ugly uglier ugliest recording and playback is with counterrecording and playback   the first step is to isolate and cut association lines of the control machine carry a tape recorder with you and record all the ugliest stupidest things cut your ugly tapes in together speed up slow down play backwards inch the tape   you will hear one ugly voice and see one ugly spirit is made of ugly old prerecordings   the more you run the tapes through and cut them up the less power they will have   cut the prerecordings into air into thin air